I0551492

THE LITERARY FANTASY MAGAZINE

Volume 1
Issue 2
Summer 2025

Editor-in-Chief: James D. Mills
Fiction Editor: Lee Patton
Associate Editors: Menke HB, Yackelyn Anillo
Submission Readers: Menke HB, Juliette Wallace

Contributing Authors: Cale Rubenstein, Catherine Yeates, Charlie Freelander, David Henson, DJ Tyrer, Ed Kratz, Ephraim, James C. Clar, James D. Mills, Jake Nuttall, Miles Lizak, Mica Smith, Raima Larter, Stefano Ronchi, Tony Daly, Victoria C. Roskams, and Yucheng Tao

THE ARCANIST: FANTASY PUBLISHING

The Arcanist: Fantasy Publishing, LLC

Bloomington, Indiana, United States.

Websites: thearcanist.net | magazine.thearcanist.net

Contact: business@thearcanist.net

Support: support@thearcanist.net

First paperback edition: July 2025
First ebook edition: July 2025

Paperback ISBN: 979-8-9923135-3-6
eBook ISBN: 979-8-9923135-4-3

Greetings dear readers,

Thank you for purchasing Issue 2 of *The Literary Fantasy Magazine*. We have taken painstaking measures to curate a selection of Fantasy literature that will not only entertain but also linger in the mind long after you have finished this paperback. There are a few unintentional motifs in this issue that emerged during the edit—stories about strange animals, stories in modern and futuristic settings, stories told in segments from various perspectives, and stories that straddle the line between Fantasy and Science Fiction.

If you've read our first issue, then you know we *strictly* publish Fantasy—not Sci-Fi, nor Speculative Fiction. Yet "The Pack" by Raima Larter and "Litter Life" by Stefano Ronchi at first seem to *strictly* follow conventions of Speculative Fiction. Both stories sparked debates among the staff—just what *is* a Fantasy story?

What I love about these tales is that they wear the uniform of Speculative Fiction, yet they have the bones and genetics of Fantasy. The worldview of Larter's furry characters is one of wonder and whimsy that evokes an unmistakably fantastic tone. The brilliant absurdity of Ronchi's setup and the subsequent fracturing of modern society into a fanatical theocracy closely mirrors ancient mythology and god-concerned Epic Fantasy.

I want to thank the kind folks at the Storytelling Collective. Last year, we partnered with them for their yearly Short Story September workshop, granting priority submissions to writers who completed the workshop. This was an amazing opportunity—not only did we receive our heaviest submission load of 2024, but we had the chance to publish several workshop graduates.

StoCo Founder, Ashley Warren, went out of her way to promote TLFM in our first months of operation. Without her and her team's generous support, I'm not sure our little publication would have made it off the ground.

Yet, here we are, one year later with our second issue. The Arcanist has a lot of amazing projects cooking up, folks. Thanks for sticking around. We'll make it worth your while.

Sincerely,

James D. Mills
Editor-in-Chief
The Arcanist: Fantasy Publishing

Congratulations to the Short Story September graduates who made it through our rigorous submission cycle:

- Alex Ward, author of "The Weight of a Torch" on our blog, which has since been expanded into a full-length novella releasing later in 2025.

- Alli Miller, author of "The Wizard's Wife" on our blog, which has since been adapted to audio.

- Cale Rubenstein, author of "After the Dragon" in this issue.

- Mica Smith, author of "A Dress Made of Magic" in this issue.

- Miles Lizak, author of "Lead Collectors" in this issue.

- Stefano Ronchi, author of "Litter Life" in this issue.

CONTENTS

In order of appearance

Flash Fiction

Short Fiction

Poetry

Serial Fiction

Interior Art

OF OSIRIS, DIONYSOS, BACHHASS, OR MOSES
By Tony Daly

I held golden rays of morning sun,
caught them rebounding off
rippling river's surface
with hands—delicate, chubby.
I thought of freedom,
of independence,
of the loving arms holding my frail body,
quivering, laden with sobs and prayers.

I was silent as she pleaded for forgiveness,
forgiveness for giving me life,
for being unworthy of my love,
of my responsibility,
for what she had to do.

The river was crackling radiance
as I felt the rough embrace
of a reed basket.
I silently watched her
standing on river bank,
partially obscured by swaying reeds,
until she was stolen by shadow and fog.

I heard the river turn red,
and angry men cursing her name.

I lay in nature's womb,
waiting to be reborn—again,
I forgave her,
but for them, I knew
the flow of time would bring me back
to these red shores.

THE LEAD COLLECTORS
By Miles Lizak

They arrive in the still hours before dawn, when a crisp chill hovers low over the earth, poised to condense into dew. Swaying points of light appear in the darkness between the pines and resolve themselves into oil lanterns, carried by silent figures. They emerge from the forest in a steady wave, intent but unhurried, and spread into the field.

With pails slung at their hips, the figures move among the low, dark mounds that rise out of the trampled grass. Leaning over the mounds, they reach into them with forceps of polished copper, pluck out little globs of lead, and drop them—*plunk*—into their pails.

A mother with a bundle swaddled to her back nudges a splayed arm with her bare foot. She crouches beside the corpse to pick up a flat metal box. As she stands, she tests the torpedo-shaped capsule at the top. She hands the box to one of the eager-eyed children who carry waterskins among the gatherers. He dutifully runs back to deliver it to the circle of blankets where the old women work. Gnarled fingers slide capsules out and disassemble them—shuck off the bright casings, pour out the black dust inside, and pop the point of lead into the wide bowl in the center of the circle. *Plunk, plunk.*

Soon, the field echoes with it, the tinkle of the harvest into tin pails.

When the mother's pail is heavy, she turns toward the workshop pitched in the shadow of the pines, where the alchemists lean over their work and apprentices stoke the stove fires. She empties the pellets into a basin of water, which a broad, bare-chested man stirs with a wooden paddle. The water is dark with blood—the man motions for the next harvester to wait while he strains out the lead globes and pours in fresh water.

An apprentice deposits the washed metal into the alchemist's cauldron—a heavy iron pan etched with symbols that describe the essence of all things. The alchemist's hands move in a practiced sequence over the lead as it melts into a dull, viscous liquid. Her cracked lips form the shapes of words but make no human sound. She lowers her head, and as she exhales a long breath over the cauldron, the light reflecting upwards onto her face turns bright and golden. She pours the liquid into sand molds to harden into small, round cakes that they will trade with the strangers.

Someone lays a hand on her shoulder. The alchemist looks up and smiles. She calls to the man working over the next stove—he waves a hand without looking up—and rises, gathering up a corner of her tunic to wipe her brow. She accepts a drink of water and kisses the glowing woman who brought it.

At the other side of the field, a gurgling cry in a stranger's tongue. A young harvester draws away from the writhing shape on the ground, his hand moves from the knife at his belt to his canteen, to the strap that might be used as a tourniquet. But the older harvester beside him puts out a hand and shakes his head. The younger one turns to argue, but sees in his elder's expression the empathy behind the cold resolution. He takes the spring-box from the dying soldier's weapon, drops the empty remains, and turns away.

The other marks the spot in his mind—to return when the bleeding stops.

Nuclear Tides
By Jake Nuttall

They lived beneath the oceans, at impossible, nightmare depths. As the millennia separated them from the races of man, they dove deeper and deeper, and in their underwater cities, the mer developed extraordinary societies of art, culture, and technological advancement.

They tapped into the nature of the blessed hydrogen molecule that had made all life on this planet possible. They forged power plants of immeasurable magnitude, pouring out hot fission energy. These enabled them to develop to their utmost pinnacle. They built branching highways of currents and electricity. They lit up the depths of the blackest ocean. They read the ancestry of the megalodons in the swirling sharks.

But for all this, they still did not see the danger boiling at the base of their cities, waiting to be unleashed in a series of poorly timed decisions on the part of Friyu Redclan, an operator at the Me'yun fission station, central Galpole, Western Anem.

The station sent heat and energy into five million homes and three million businesses, all collated under billions of conch-shell wire casings and tubes of clean gas, spinning and rotating back to the great ammonite shell housing the power plant.

Friyu punched the coolant tubes, letting the central chamber flood with ice-cold seawater. The resonator roiled and hissed, sending out hot vibrations through the air to fog up the twelve feet of solid glass that formed the barrier between the central burner and Friyu's observation deck. The scalloped, clam-like encasement protected him, but if the reactor burned too hot, they risked a radiation leak. Too cold, and the engine might revert to a dull core. After that, it would take ages to get it burning and emitting normally.

But Galpole's leaders would not accept such a lack of efficiency. Outages were punished; sometimes with trench duty, sometimes with public humiliation. If he let the site hiccup, even for a moment, Friyu risked exposing his clan name to these consequences. That, he could not accept.

He watched the gauges, indicated by globules floating between gradual measurements, and kept his eyes alert and bouncing between the tubes. He had done this every day for the last three years. The job had become so married to his consciousness, even his dreams brimmed with pipes, bubbles, and the rippling sound radiating off each of the core indicators. When he fell into it—really lost himself in the work—he was practically an extension of his instruments, the levers balancing easily in his deft, pale fingers.

But not when his supervisor, Frehr Rire, was around. In Rire's presence, Friyu had a tendency to slip awkwardly at the lever. He had just done so and overcorrected, pushing the temperature gauge too far down. A blue undercurrent flooded the chamber above them. Friyu got it back up to a solid tread, and the color returned to a pulsing white-yellow. The electric air hummed pleasantly.

"You losing it, Redclan?" said Rire, his voice rolling hot off Friyu's shoulders and back.

"No, sir. I am operating in flow. You startled me, is all."

"And what about me should startle you?" Rire asked.

The mer's luminescent yellow eyes constricted to tight pinpricks. Friyu felt a fresh wave of loathing for his boss.

"Nothing at all, sir," he said.

"Because what's startling are those trends in the thermal readouts," said Rire. "Have you seen how high we've spiked over the last fourteen tides? It'll look like we mean to insult the Hierarchies if something happens out here. A current gets irradiated, a minnow gets fried…. It's on our gills, you get me?"

Friyu looked into the mer's leering, beady-eyed face and nodded.

He found himself scanning every bubble in the readout, every holographic map of temperatures and flows. His fingers slid and bounced on the instruments on his shelf-rock dashboard. His people were not astronomers, but their logic deduced the nature of the celestial bodies all the same. He knew what power lay there, how it could warm and light and burn and mutilate and kill. He was well aware of the dangers.

So when the last module rose to a high red in its cylinder, Friyu Redclan flipped six of the fourteen stalks and twisted the ammonite spiral that composed the shutdown procedure.

And yet the procedure—designed to be infallible—failed.

The valves dispensed and brought a whole torrent of ice-cold seafloor water crashing down into the nuclear generator. Still, it burned so hot and so bright that it melted the shell of tempered glass between them, all twelve feet of it. Friyu was gone in seconds, but it would have pleased him to know that his supervisor followed shortly after.

The bulbous gases and toxic fumes rose in an enveloping cloud, eradicating all life within a 300-square-mile area of Galpole. Twenty million merfolk died instantly. The radiation made it all the way to the surface, where it triggered the military sirens of every major nation on every continent in the human world.

Above the surface, no one knew who had set off the bomb, only that it had to be a bomb.

Naturally, this meant that every nation had an impugnable *casus belli*. Someone was out there, carelessly flaunting nuclear weapons, and the funny thing about carelessness is that it tends to be contagious. Soon, everyone itched for the chance to get careless with a nuclear weapon.

The first bombs that fell on land did not target any major cities. Instead, they were intended to test the waters. Annapolis and Lviv went up, then Qods and Guadalajara. From there, the major population centers fell like dominoes.

Underwater, meanwhile, the radiation seeped in from every angle, currents mutated, burning, and sick. The remaining Anems went to war. Death reigned, and societal collapse mirrored the world above.

Together, the worlds of men and mer died, and neither kind ever knew a thing about the other.

1939

By Yucheng Tao

When I was a child,
on a small island, I was there, remembering.
In the attic, a black book cloaked in dust—
I found it.

A strange mist leaped off its pages,
speaking with glee:
"I carry the prophecy of your end."

I didn't know why it chose me to tell it.
"I am trapped, a Prophet for centuries.
Thank you for freeing me.
I give you the gift of prophecy:
you shall survive beyond WWII."

"I would
die
before the war."

In a world where sanity slips away,
I would see sense as hell,
and face the frenzied abyss.

I was afraid.

1939 has arrived.

HUNT'S END
By DJ Tyrer

Germany. Of course, it was Germany. Was it mocking him, bringing him back to a place he had no desire to revisit, or did it thrive on the echoes of the horrors that had happened there? Things he wished not to remember. Either way, it was his duty to destroy it, and this was where the trail had led them, where the hunt would end, at last.

Joseph felt out of place in the glass-built tower block, holding a curved sword like a sickle that he had made himself. It had taken him years to learn the craft, but then he had the time. Time was the only thing he had. Perhaps had he held a gun, it might not have seemed so strange, the merging of past and present that reminded him he didn't belong in this world.

He glanced at his daughter. Awa walked parallel to him, an identical sword in her hand. Her skin was several shades darker than his, an inheritance from her mother, long dead in what was now South Sudan. She returned his look with an expression of greater certainty than he felt.

Awa crouched. "Father."

He looked where she was pointing. A splash of slime, dark and viscous. If only it would leave a slug-like path for them to follow. Not for the first time, he wondered exactly what it looked like. It felt strange to have hunted it for so long, to share such ties with it, and not know what form it took.

He straightened his back. "Come on."

Their footsteps echoed about them as they ascended the stairs, checking every floor in turn. There was no power, no elevators, but the sunlight streamed through the glass walls, illuminating much of the building's interior. He carried a flashlight to shine into the dark corners of the inner rooms, examining the shifting shadows for any hint of danger.

It was like walking through a nightmare. The sword shook in his hand. The one Awa held never so much as twitched. Joseph had never been a warrior, nor any kind of hero. If he were honest with himself, he was a coward. A bit of a bully once. Able only to pick on those weaker than him, making himself feel bigger. No longer. Now, he was just left with fear.

He would have happily turned and run for it, but his fear of leaving the job undone was greater than the fear of what he faced. Yet, there were some things he would much rather not confront. Awa showed no sign of such doubts.

"It's here somewhere," he said, unwilling to name it or even invest it with real identity. It was just a thing, nothing more, unworthy of continued life.

Awa snorted at his words. Of course, it was. They had spent long enough tracking it, following its trail of vile crimes across continents, small children slaughtered.

"I don't fear him," his daughter said.

"You should."

She snorted again.

"I have been in castles and dungeons in my time," he said, shining a beam of light into a cupboard, "and, though this reminds me of those, this is something else entirely. I feel… exposed."

Through the outer walls of the building, the open expanse of the sky was visible. As usual, mankind was reaching for Heaven. Only here, he would have to confront his own personal hell.

There was a tittering laugh, oddly muffled. He couldn't tell where it was coming from. Wherever he looked, all he saw was emptiness beyond the glass walls, room after room of nothing.

"Where is it?" Awa asked. "Is it invisible?"

"Anything is possible, I suppose," he replied. "There aren't exactly any guidelines for what we face."

He saw movement. "There!"

It was gone. Joseph muttered an old Aramaic imprecation: As the shape moved behind a pane of glass, it vanished from his sight.

"Father?"

"I think…" He tried to collect his thoughts. "I think it cannot be seen through glass. Don't ask me how…"

Memories surfaced unbidden, the stinging pain of lacerated flesh, swirling shards of crystal… Perhaps it had an affinity with glass. No wonder it had chosen the empty tower block!

"This may be more difficult than we thought," he told her.

Awa spat. "We never thought it would be easy, Father."

"No…" Not easy at all.

He led the way in the direction he thought it disappeared, eyes flickering constantly left and right, searching. He couldn't see it, but the tittering laugh continued to torment him.

"Where are you? Show yourself."

The laugh fell silent, and though he strained to hear sounds of movement, he could hear nothing. The floor might as well have been empty.

"There." Awa jabbed the point of her sword to their right, and he followed after her in pursuit, but, still, it was invisible, hidden behind the glass.

Joseph sighed and almost laughed. "Not for the first time, I cannot see what should be clear before me…"

"Ever the pessimist, Father." Despite being unable to see their quarry, Awa continued to move with confidence.

"I long ago realised that there was little in this world to be positive about."

"You need to find faith. It surprises me," she spun around the end of a glass divider and let out a frustrated cry, "that despite having evidence, you lack faith, Father."

"One is the past, the other the future. I—" Movement. "There." He sped through a gap between the glass panes into another open-plan office.

He swore. Behind him, Awa said something in her mother's language.

They had assumed that its ability to move unseen, to hide, and to target children all betokened, all betokened something small. Now, he realised that the killings represented a cruel form of revenge. It was big—bigger than him—and moved like someone tied within a duvet cover.

If anything could kill him before his time, it was this. He felt a shiver of fear run through him. Long had he hoped for death, but now…

It reared on one end, towering over them. Viscous fluid shimmered across the surface of its all-enveloping caul and dripped from it like blood. A face pressed against the fleshy cocoon from the inside, a vague hint of features, and limbs bulged out from within.

Bile rose in his throat. It reminded him of a child torn untimely from the womb. Again, memories returned: the consummation of a shameful desire, lacerating pain, and burning passion. It disgusted him to see his child before him. Laughter escaped from within the caul. Fluid dribbled off it.

"Father. Sister."

Joseph could barely keep hold of his sword in his trembling hand. He glanced at his daughter and watched even her iron resolve falter. He knew he must disgust her.

It laughed again.

"You do not want to kill me, Father," it gasped and gurgled, voice muffled. "You seek to judge me, but it is you who were judged. My sin is your sin, Father. I am what you made me. You know what it is to be beyond the bounds of mortal existence."

The sword slipped from Joseph's fingers. It was true. No man could wander the world alone, unloved, forever. And, as he learned with Awa's mother, love for a mortal brought on a special kind of pain. While she went to her just reward, he continued to wait for the second coming of the one he had struck and the uncertainty of judgement. Only with another like himself could he find an equal companionship. A fool to himself, he had been easy prey for a succubus. His son was his sin manifested.

It flopped down and spasms ran along its length as it gyrated towards them, as if seeking a vile embrace.

"No…" Joseph was frozen.

Calling out to God, Awa leapt towards her hideous half-sibling, swinging her sword as if she were harvesting grain. The blade sliced through the caul, tearing a gash along its length. Bloody fluid rushed out of it, and it deflated like a popped balloon. A disgusting smell washed over them, like rotten meat.

There was a sickening, gurgling scream, and his son slid out of it. It was human in general shape, but the proportions were not quite right. But, it was its skin… His son was made of glass or crystal, the surface of the clouded blue substance stained with fluid.

Joseph cried out in horror. "God forgive me."

Awa didn't hesitate. She swung her sword down in a mighty blow, striking her half-brother. It shattered into a thousand fragments with one final scream. The nearest glass partitions shattered, too.

Joseph shielded his eyes as a strangled sob escaped his lips. Fluid, caul, and glass all began to bubble and transform into a faint mist, the stench growing even more overpowering. He turned away. When he dared look again, his son was gone. All that was left was a faint stain upon the floor.

"My sin…" he murmured.

His daughter stepped over to him and patted his arm.

"Father, you've lived fifty lifetimes, yet have not sinned fifty times as much as mortal men."

He shook his head. "No matter."

"Well, now, one less hangs over you…"

Joseph didn't feel as if a weight had been lifted from him. Perhaps he never would.

He jabbed his thumb at his chest. "I cannot escape my worst sin. No others matter."

Awa shrugged. "Is that God's judgment or your own guilt?"

He looked away, wishing he knew the answer.

A Memory To Forget

by David Henson

"Just one? I thought it was three. And it's supposed to be wishes."

He rolls his eyes. He wears black jeans and a red T-shirt. He's bald and has a gold hoop in his right ear. "That's Hollywood Bollywood BS," he says. "I'm granting you one forgotten memory, Kenneth. That there's the real deal, my friend." He stretches backwards. "Oh, that feels good."

"You been cooped up in a lamp?"

"As I said — Hollywood Bollywood."

He puts his hand on my shoulder just as he did when he *poofed* into my living room. Once again, his touch evaporates my suspicion. I go to the mantle and pick up the framed photo of Elizabeth and me with our daughter, Cynthia. We're all beaming because Cynthia just won her school's mathlete competition. "You could make me forget the most painful memory of my life?"

"If you want to forget about your wife's death, I can make that happen, Kenny-boy."

"How did you know I was—"

"I'm a pro. I do my homework."

"I'll remember our 32 years together? But not her death?"

"Bingo, buddy. But I suggest you think it through. Let me help." He touches my shoulder.

I'm awash with thoughts that are mine but not mine, seeing a man that's me, but not me, calling my daughter.

Hi, Cynthia.

How are you today, Dad?

Honey, I can't find your mother. Is she over there? I'm getting really worried.

Cynthia sighs. Oh, Dad. Mom passed away, remember?

She … what? The man drops the phone and sinks to his knees.

I feel a hand lift from my shoulder. "I'd forget my wife's death, but I have to relive it all over again. I guess you're one of those genies who twist wishes into nightmares."

He shakes his head. "If I were one of those SOBs, I wouldn't have given you that preview. I do this because… I have to." He takes a deep breath. "So, what do you want to forget? Careful. No more sneak peeks."

I recall the time I struck out in **Little League** with the bases loaded. All the taunts and boos.

"You quit your childish dream of being a major leaguer after that and buckled down in school," he says.

"Will forgetting that—"

"Memories are threads, Kenny. Cut one, and the pattern stays, but the texture? The weave? Who knows?"

"I have no idea what that means."

He rolls his eyes and shakes his head. "Forgetting that memory won't change your life up to now. But you'll be a different butterfly, so in the future…" He shrugs. "Ready?" He starts to snap his fingers.

I grab his hand. "Hold on."

I think of the day I got passed over for a promotion. I quit and opened my bookshop. No regrets. Another image flares in my mind. "I was broken-hearted when Fluffy passed, but I don't want to relive her death over and over. Can—"

"Ah, pets." His lips twitch. "So fleeting." He clears his throat. "But not so complex. I could make you forget you ever had Fluffy."

I picture her rubbing against my legs, purring on my lap. "Give me another minute."

"Mortals. Always so slow. I could grow a beard waiting for your decision." Suddenly, he has a goatee.

There must be something I want to expunge. A regret, an unkindness. But everything I think of is intertwined with something I don't want to forget. Everything but one. I tell him what I've decided.

He smiles. "Finally, I've found someone who understands. Now I can move on." He snaps his fingers.

* * *

"Hello, Cynthia."

"How are you feeling today, Dad?"

"I've been looking all morning. I couldn't find... my reading glasses."

My daughter chuckles. "I bet you had them pushed up on your forehead again."

"You know me as well as your mother did. Funny thing. I have a vague recollection of a visit from a strange man this morning. Just can't remember."

"A dream?"

"I don't think so. Anyway... I've been thinking about that time you won the math contest."

AFTER THE DRAGON
By Cale Rubenstein

From the balcony of the royal chambers, Will had a perfect view of the makeshift tribunal assembled in the courtyard. A centuries-old table and chair had been dragged out from the dining hall that morning, the gilt chipping as they pulled it screeching across marble floors. The furniture loomed in the center of the square, waiting for the judge and the prisoner. A mass of rebels lined the walls, most of them commoners clutching rusty weapons and farming tools. It had been one week since they stormed the palace, and the day had finally come for the king to face judgment. But it was already late afternoon, and Will's father was still hidden away.

The crowd was restless, their murmuring angry and impatient, the sounds twisting Will's stomach. He exhaled and forced himself to release his grip on the railing. "They'll bring us down there soon," he thought out loud. "If they hate the monarchy as much as they say, we'll be on trial right alongside Father."

From his right, his mother snorted, a sound unbecoming of a royal lady, known for her legendary beauty and elegance. "They didn't come for us," she said, unworried. She had remained her typical unflappable self their entire imprisonment—it was admirable, if not incredibly infuriating. "We're not the ones who impoverished the populace, or burned down their villages, or caused a famine with sheer incompetence." She straightened in her chair and peered over the balustrade. "They'll let us go when this is over."

Will bristled at each accusation. He had heard them, and worse, in the last few days. Ever since the rebels had broken through the gates— supposedly impenetrable gates—there was no end to talk of the king's cruelty. It was as if the uprising had kicked over a rock, spilling all of his father's ugliness into the light.

"Well then, what's going to happen to *him?*" Will snapped.

She thinned her lips. "In this case? It's hard to say. Historically, when a ruler is deposed, it's by a relative or some other nation, and they take over succession." Her eyes flitted to Will. "In those scenarios, they often execute the heir. So perhaps, be grateful."

Will ignored the jab, returning his gaze to the courtyard. He glanced across at the door to their chambers, feeling the inside of his coat, his mind turning over countless half-crazed plots for rescuing his family. He knew there were orders to keep them unharmed, but that couldn't last.

The crowd raged, shouting their hunger for the king. Will had no idea where his father was being held; images of him chained to the wall in a dungeon or thrown into a hole flooded his mind.

As always, his mother seemed to hear Will's thoughts. "You know, he was only a couple of years older than you when we wed." She waved her hand, flicking away the memory. "Some idiot peasant with a sword and a magic ring kills a dragon. A month later, your grandfather names him heir to the throne and just gives me away."

Will scoffed, exasperation pushing aside other thoughts. "You speak of being grateful, Mother. As I recall from the bards, Father had rescued *you* from that dragon." Will knew it was more complicated than that—there had been an evil magician and talking sparrow and a slew of other things only hinted at in the stories—but it was a reflex to defend his father. Will doubted that it would ever go away.

She raised an eyebrow, and he resisted the urge to squirm beneath her scrutiny. "And a penchant for violence and cruelty makes for a good king?" she responded coolly. "I spent my entire childhood in the palace library, learning laws, science, and language. All for your father to ignore me these last seventeen years, content only with a crown and an heir."

Will opened his mouth, but the rebuttal died on his tongue. They've had this conversation countless times, even before their imprisonment. And she was right. Pushed aside, his mother had focused her time on educating Will. "If I do nothing else," she would say, "I'll make sure there is never another king like your father."

Will felt a pang of shame, whether on behalf of himself or his father, he wasn't sure. Had he worn a blindfold his entire life, or did he just refuse to see the truth? Will was no fool. He never claimed his father was a *good* king. Or even a good father, if he was being honest. And obviously, he wasn't a good husband. Even so, he couldn't place this new, sinister picture of his father alongside the memories of horse riding and hunting lessons, or his shouting encouragement from the walls as Will trained with the knights.

His brooding was interrupted by a tug on his shirt. "Will, I'm *bored*," a small voice said behind him. "Can we play a game?"

Turning, he smiled despite himself at the sight of his younger sister. "Not right now, Gabrielle." He handed her his empty scabbard; his sword had been taken the night they were captured. "Why don't you see if there are any monsters hiding in here?"

Gabrielle squealed with delight, raising the scabbard over her head triumphantly and running into the bedroom. His mother's eyes followed, not attempting to conceal her disapproval. Will ignored her, too happy to watch his sister poke at the shadows under the bed. He may have felt loyalty towards his father and respect for his mother, but Will's love for his sister outshone them all, as it had since the day she was born, nearly five years ago.

There was a soft rapping from the far side of the bedroom, and his heart jumped. "I'll get that," he muttered. It took everything not to run to the door leading to the hallway. He opened it to find a servant holding a plate of food.

"Your midday meal, m'lord," the servant said, holding a tray and lowering his head. Will's fingers twitched, desperate to pull the man inside. It was Oliver.

The guard posted at the door hauled Oliver upright. "You don't need to grovel to the likes of him anymore," he said, smirking at Will. "He's nothing now."

Will attempted to cloak himself in the affect of his mother. "And yet," Will replied. "Here you are, forced to keep watch on me. How does it feel to betray your country and play wet nurse?"

The guard's face turned stormy; he grabbed Will's tunic, pulling him close. His breath reeked of wine—probably one of their better vintages. "If I could, I'd break both your arms and throw you off that balcony."

Will managed to keep a blank expression as he gingerly removed the guard's hands. "But you can't, can you?" he said. "You're not allowed. So get back to work." Not looking away, he reached for the door and swung it shut.

Will's knees buckled as soon as the latch clicked. He admonished himself for being afraid. What kind of man is terrified of a single drunk rebel? But he couldn't help it; the exchange stirred up memories of that first night: the doors of his room slamming open, the certainty he was going to die at the hands of the disheveled group pulling him to his feet. Instead, they only carried him down the hall and threw him into the royal chambers with his mother and sister. The servants had remained unharmed, thankfully, bringing food and fresh linens. It was they who had first warned Will of the roiling battles between rebels and loyalists raging through the country. And it was among them that Will found someone who could help.

"You shouldn't provoke him," Oliver warned, as they moved deeper into the foyer of the chambers. "He's a menace. The rest of the staff are terrified of him."

"He's an idiot," Will replied. "Which is why he has never thought to search any of you. Did you find it?"

Oliver adopted an ingratiating smile, placing the tray on a table and lifting a cover off a bowl. At the bottom of the dish was a battered silver ring, patterned with a thread of green stone. "The vault was just where you said it was." He bowed, presenting the ring to Will.

"Praise the gods." Will exhaled, a knot in his chest loosening, and picked up the ring. "And thank you. I know what a risk it was to retrieve this."

Oliver's smile deepened. "I live to serve the crown."

"Of course," Will said, rolling his eyes. He felt inside his coat and pulled out a necklace, studded with rubies and emeralds. "That should be enough for your own palace somewhere."

The jewelry disappeared into Oliver's clothes before Will realized it had left his hand, and the next moment the servant had dashed back out the door, a few words of thanks lingering in the air.

Will placed the ring in his pocket. His relief disappeared as he remembered he still had no idea how to use it. Ever since Oliver agreed to smuggle it for him, Will had been racking his mind for some plan to save his family, but he had nothing.

There was a yelp and crash from another room. "Mama, Will," Gabrielle called out, "I broke something."

Will found her next to a pile of shattered glass, eyes downcast. Whatever it had been before its encounter with Gabrielle, it had been expensive.

"I didn't mean to knock it over," she said, as she handed Will back his scabbard. "I was swinging at the drapes."

He bent down and began to gently sweep the glass into a pile. "It's okay," he said. "It was ugly anyway. Just don't walk over here."

She jumped into a nearby chair and swung her legs, the destruction already forgotten. "When do you think we can leave?" she asked.

"What?" Will teased. "You don't like all of us sleeping in the same room?"

Gabrielle's expression turned serious. "No, your breath smells in the morning," she said seriously, before collapsing in a series of giggles.

"Is that so?" Will said, ruffling her hair. "Well, you snore."

He rose, took a few steps towards the balcony.

"Will?" The concern in his sister's voice caught him mid-stride. "Are we going to be okay?"

Every muscle seemed to clench. "Of course," he assured, kneeling so their eyes met. "I promise nothing will happen to us."

"How do you know?" Gabrielle insisted.

He glanced behind his shoulder and gave her a half-smile. "Can you keep a secret?"

"Of course," she chirped, the worry in her voice disappearing. "Tell me, tell me."

He reached inside his coat and pulled the ring out of his pocket. "Do you know what this is?"

She squinted. "It's just an old ring."

"No," he grinned, lowering his voice. "It's a wishing ring. It transports you to anywhere you want, as long as you know exactly where you're going."

Gabrielle gasped. "Just like the one father used to get into the dragon's lair!"

"The very same," Will said. "And if the time comes, I'll give it to you and you can wish us to our cousin's castle. You remember where that is?" Their cousin was married to a duke of an allied nation, far away from the chaos consuming the country.

"I remember, it's the one by the lake." She peered at the ring, as if she could see the enchantment coursing through it. She frowned, and her voice dropped to a hush. "I heard one of the servants say Father is a bad king. They said he's evil. That's why all these people came and are keeping us here." Her lip trembled..

Will hesitated, unsure how to respond. "Father did his best," he said at last. "It's hard, being a king." Will wrapped his arms around her. "When this is over, let's go out to the country. We can ride horses, and I'll show you how to shoot a bow and arrow."

She nodded against his shoulder, and he could feel the tears dampening his shirt. "Come on, I'll read to you," he said, picking her up and carrying her to the bed. He sat next to her, pulling a worn book from the floor and beginning from where they had stopped last night. Within minutes, she was asleep.

He slid his way out of the bed, a pang of guilt striking as he crept towards the balcony. What Will didn't tell his sister was that the wishing ring only worked for whoever was wearing it. He would give the ring to Gabrielle over anyone else, but that would be the last resort.

Will gently closed the door behind him when he reached the balcony. The scene below remained unchanged. His mother looked at him in question.

"She's okay. Scared, of course."

She nodded, her face softening in a way only Will could see. "I'm glad she's had you in her life. It's hard, being the daughter of a king."

Will cocked his head. But he wasn't able to ask more. As if summoned by her words, they led his father into the courtyard, his arms bound behind his back, crown still resting on his head. A rebel shoved him to his knees when he reached the front of the table.

At the same time, a man emerged from the grand hall, striding towards the king like a wolf towards a deer with a broken leg. Will recognized him, and a wave of bile rose in his throat. It was the leader of the rebellion.

"Your majesty," the man boomed, with all the revelry of an actor performing on stage. "Because of you, our people have been murdered, starved, jailed, and forced into destitution. With your illegitimate rule, you have brought our country to ruin. While you have feasted behind these walls, we have starved!" The crowd jeered, and the man pointed at the king. "For these crimes, and all the crimes not spoken of today, you are charged with treason. How do you respond?"

Will silently begged his father to show humility, to beg for mercy and forgiveness, and agree to cede power.

"Treason," his father spat, his voice grated and strained. "Filth. I am the king. You will all hang for this." Will groaned and put his head in his hands. It had been a foolish hope.

"You *were* the king," the man corrected, sitting in the chair. "Now, you are nothing." He made a signal, and another person stepped forward, ripping off the crown and stomping on it to the cheers of the crowd. "Believe me," the rebel leader continued, "this brings me no pleasure. You were one of us, born among the mud and filth. We thought you'd protect us, bring upon a new era."

His father's face was grotesque with contempt as he stared at the mangled crown. "I was never anything like you."

The air grew thick and feverish as the crowd yelled curses and beat their feet against the floor. Some threw stones. Will reached into his coat and grasped the ring.

"The era of kings is over," the man shouted, speaking to the crowd now, voice rising above the noise. "This is the beginning of a new age. Of reason and laws and justice."

Will jumped to his feet, unable to stand the hypocrisy any longer. "This isn't justice, this is vengeance!" he shouted, the sound swallowed up by the clamor below.

"Be quiet," his mother said, grabbing his coat and pulling him down to his chair. Her lips curve into a knowing smile.

"You're enjoying this?" Will asked in disbelief. "Do you really hate Father that much?"

She turned to him, eyes resolute. "Of course I do. You know that. But it's not just your father. Or my father. Or even my grandfather, who I never knew, but I'm sure committed some atrocity. It's all of it." She swept her arm over the palace, its colonnades and walls, and parapets. "It's this place. It's a cycle. It corrupts. And now I won't see that happen to you."

The leader leapt atop the table, drawing Will back to the turmoil below. "And it won't stop," he yelled. "Every duke, every earl, every baron—they will give up their titles. Their land will be ours, the stones of their castles will build our homes, the furs of their coats will keep our children warm." He pointed to Will's father. "And you, my friend, will have the ignominious fate of being our last king."

Will stood, the ring digging into his hand. He started to slip it onto his finger, but paused. He needed to wait for the right moment.

"What should we do with him?" the leader cried. The crowd yelled all sorts of punishments. The man raised his arms and spun in a circle, basking in their discontent. And for one, almost imperceptible moment, the rebel paused and looked at the balcony. Shocked, Will pulled his hand from his coat.

But the rebel wasn't looking at him. From the corner of his eye, Will saw his mother nod.

"I say… to death goes the king," the man bellowed. The crowd roared its approval and took up the cry. "To death goes the king, to death goes the king." But their chants fell to a buzz as Will rounded on his mother.

"It was *you*," Will flared. "You're working with the rebels. You helped them break into the palace. That's why they won't hurt us. All of this is your fault."

"No," his mother said, rising and meeting his eyes. She pointed to his father, struggling while the rebel leader forced him over a block of wood. "It's his fault. He had his chance. And once he's gone, I can do some good and help this country."

Will gestured to the frenzied courtyard. "And this is the country you seek? How are you any better than he is?"

Her eyes narrowed. "Tyranny can only die, not change. New eras are born in blood. My lessons should have taught you that."

"Well, I won't sit back and watch it happen." Will's choice was simple now. Gabrielle and his mother would be safe thanks to whatever perfidious arrangement she had made. Will pulled out the wishing ring.

His mother inhaled sharply. "What are you doing?"

The crowd roared as a man emerged, brandishing an ax. "What do you think?" Will snapped, slipping the ring onto his finger. "I'm going to wish myself down there and give Father the ring. He can use it to send himself somewhere safe."

"Idiot," his mother hissed, grabbing his wrist. "They'll kill you, and I won't be able to stop them. And then what happens? He'll lead an army right back here and be more vicious than ever before."

Will snatched his hand away. "You don't know that. And it doesn't matter. I can't just let him die!" He put the ring on his finger, bringing it to his lips.

She grabbed his shirt, pulling him down to face her. "*Stop*. Listen to me. You don't care about this country or its people, or even yourself? Fine. But if your father remains king, what do you think happens to your sister?"

Will hesitated. The courtyard clamored as the headsman sauntered towards the king, slowed by the crowd clasping his shoulder and patting him on the back. "What do you mean?"

Her eyes bored into his. "I told you, it's a cycle. You'll be gone, and there will be no heir. Your sister will be married off, just like I was. And you know your father. Tell me, do you think it will be to someone kind and compassionate?"

Will froze. A dread, stronger than anything he had felt in the last week, rose up to his throat. "He wouldn't do that," he whispered. The roars from the mob grew, a cavalcade that threatened to sweep him away.

She held his gaze. "I thought the same thing about my father."

The certainty of her words collapsed on top of him, crushing him against the cries from below. She was right, she was always right. His mother was saying something else, but he couldn't hear her. The headsman was only a few steps from his father. Will took off the ring and forced himself to keep his eyes open.

When the ax fell, he collapsed, his mother's hand on his shoulder.

THE BAPTISM OF THE PETIT COMTE
By Victoria C. Roskams

It was a strange fancy of the Count's to suddenly order that his son be baptised, but then he had had many a strange fancy before.

It ill became him to live in England, Louis thought. Since they had set foot on its shores – Louis for the first time, his master making a return after some years – a pall-like whiteness had begun its descent over Count Eric Stenbock, beginning with his hands and creeping upwards, upwards, spreading itself over the contours of his long, thin face. Yet he possessed such thought, such care for others, in the midst of all this wasting. Daily, Stenbock turned his face, his eyes seeming to see death waiting in the wings, towards one or other of his two servants, and asked after the health of his son. The Petit Comte was paramount. Supine, maiden-like in the enclosure of red walls and numerous shawls brought over from India, Stenbock extended a peremptory arm and asked for his son. It happened this way every morning (they must, in concession to his ways, consider the morning as extending at least until three in the afternoon). But this morning it happened thus:

"Alfred, bring me the Petit Comte. I fear his end approaches, and I will not have him leave this world unbaptised."

The strangest of fancies, but they must all be indulged. Here, amid the shawls, an icon of the Buddha nestled alongside a bust of Shelley, intersected by a crucifix; forms of worship jostled. Eros stood erect and alone in bronze, untwined from Psyche. The oddness, the singularity, must be allowed and discreetly ignored. With a nod, Fred exited the bedchamber.

"My dear Louis," continued Stenbock, an arm dallying in midair, "I have a mind to ask you to fetch Solomon."

"Solomon, sir?" said Louis.

"Simeon, you know, of art fame, of dear friend fame. Yes, I think I will ask you to bring me Solomon."

An eyebrow-raise might have been perceptible to an onlooker, had not the room been shrouded in an artificially nocturnal gloom by heavy velvet hangings across the slit window. "Mr Solomon, sir," Louis began hesitantly, "has been in the workhouse these last few years." He considered. "He is a drunkard, sir." Better not to linger with held tongue over such nastiness.

"Yes, yes," came the hurried reply from the bed, "now do go and fetch him."

The Count would get these ideas and notions. Louis supposed it was all that lying down all day, doing nothing but thinking. As for himself, Louis stood all day, doing nothing but thinking: he found the standing made all the difference. "Very well, sir," he said, and with an obliging swoop, left the room.

Might Stenbock draw the curtain and suffuse the room with the light now begging to enter –? But no, before long, there would be candles. Stenbock brought a finger before his eyes and imagined its lithe lengths tapering like a wick. It was an alleviation, after all, to reflect on how many candles he had burned. In his life, the altar had never been left unattended, unlit, for even a moment. A life lived to the lees –! But then it was not he who was waning, he must remember, but his dear son and heir. And, oh! he had always meant to take his leave first, after bestowing on the boy an enviable collection of items sacred, profane, and arcane, not to mention a wardrobe bursting with silk blouses. From such a flame-like life, these mementos would be precious remnants indeed. But no: it befell him to bestow – and he reflected now on the folly of never yet having taken the opportunity – that most delicate, that most vigorous, of benisons. Not to place an object in his son's open hand, but to take him and suspend him, beautifully poised, between this world and the next, and assure his safe passage. Yet that light, clawing now around the curtain, was really most aggravating. He must set Louis on the matter upon his return. It did not do to unwittingly glow.

And there was his son, in Fred's arms, limply and mutely dangling, little knowing the blessings shortly to land upon his head.

"Bring him here."

Fred placed the doll, hardly smaller than Stenbock himself, across his master's body, stepping back discreetly from the bed as Stenbock gathered it hungrily into his arms. With caresses and murmurings, he gazed, as if lit by fire, into its eyes.

"My Stanislaus, my Stanislaus," sang Stenbock, "what ails thee? For I think I have never seen thee look so pale. It is as though the moon has stolen into my chamber, but it is thy face. Alfred, think you not he looks pale?"

Archly, the servant considered, as on many mornings before, the possibility of fluctuations of pallor in a creature assembled out of porcelain, plaster of Paris, and padding. His answer must be as unchanging, however, as the thing's state of health; therefore:

"I see no immediate cause for concern, sir."

"No –? No immediate –? But you are a worldly fellow, Alfred, you do not muse as I do on the troubled, the troubling, penumbra separating this world from the next." An ivory hand passed over a forehead of impossible smoothness, undisturbed by blemish or age. "Who can say – who can have the arrogance as to presume to say – when his hour may come? And yet I think, as the moon steals inwards, I think I see a foretelling shadow in thine eyes. I ought to have known it would be thus when I named thee Stanislaus, thinking only – selfishly – of perpetuating the name I chose on my own baptism. But thy baptism must, it shall, be today, my own Stanislaus. I have told thee the story of thy namesake –?"

Fred stood in silence, a silhouette among draped shawls. A filigree sound of wax retreating from candles tickled the air.

"Saint Stanislaus Kostka," began Stenbock solemnly – he paused, so as not to defile the name by proceeding too hastily – then began again: "Saint Stanislaus Kostka did, by the grace of God, foretell the day, the hour, and the manner of his own death." He heaved a voluble sigh, and cried: "And how was he able to do this –?!"

It was this grace, this zeal, in storytelling which had, so Louis had told Fred, made Stenbock such a favourite with the children back in Estonia.

His own Stanislaus wore a changed aspect already, Stenbock could tell: the light of rapt attention was breaking through the clouds of ill health. "There are miracles, my boy, that even the Holy Father cannot begin to fathom; events so curious, yet so perfect, in their improbability, that they must of necessity give rise to pondering throughout the ages; their mysteries unsolvable even amid the onward march of human sapience. Saint Stanislaus Kostka's death is one such miracle. He awoke one day and said it was to be so, and so it was. Nothing in his life became him so beautifully as leaving it. And he a mere seventeen years old! My dear boy, thou must learn from thy namesake that it is not the length of time one is allotted that matters, but what one makes of it. The crowning glory of his seventeen years came in those final days, in his grateful submission to God's will that he should be removed from this world and enter into blissful immortality. Yet I cannot say that I, myself, would face the certainty of the grave with such equanimity…"

Fred persisted in his silence. An air of ill-contained urgency lay behind his master's words, like a rush of water held back by floodgates. Then the storm passed; he continued in a high voice of delicate poise.

"Kostka, of course, was named for Saint Stanislaus the Martyr, a man who defeated the grave in pursuit of what was just. Did Kostka hope that he, too, might find himself resurrected, lifted by a mighty hand into eternal life? And does he not live, as surely as Saint Stanislaus the Martyr lifted the dead man from his grave? Does not he live in me, in thee –" clasping manfully his son close to his chest – "as surely as thou livest? That is the thing. Creation springs anew; it remakes the old; it lives again in new vessels, and so on and so on. It must be today, Alfred. Stanislaus must be baptised today."

Doubts must be quashed, qualms laid to rest. "Might I take the liberty, sir," asked Fred, "of suggesting that Father Pierre be found to perform the ceremony?" This was a Jesuit priest who had, for some months now, been impassively tending to the educational needs of this most unresponsive and surely unrewarding group of students.

"No," Stenbock pondered, "gratified as I have been to observe the results of Father Pierre's teachings on my son, the baptism must be performed – I feel this – by Solomon and me together. Do not ask me why; perhaps it is another of these peculiar mysteries of which we Stanislauses are so fond. You will not deplore me for eschewing the ministrations of a priest on this occasion. It must be Solomon –"

Fred gave a thought to the workhouse.

"For when I muse upon his depiction of the *Coptic Baptismal Procession* –"

Here, Stenbock gestured to the far wall, on which several framed paintings and drawings hung amid the chartreuse wallpaper; here and there a minor Millais, a rare Rossetti. An adjoining wall was given over to an exquisite collection of drawings by Aubrey Beardsley, to which the eyes of both Louis and Fred were often hopelessly drawn, diverting their gaze, then their attention, then their all-consuming thoughts – in a manner as menacing as it was titillating. But this time Fred's attention had focused on a painting of largely dim hues, accented now and then by flashes of gold, as in the tips of the thin red candles or the golden bowls held aloft by the boys at the head of the procession. They led the way, buoying the left side of the scene with their frantic excitement, while high priests swathed in capes of rich purple trooped slowly behind them. The air above them was cloudy with incense.

"It strikes me," said Stenbock dreamily, "that here is a glimpse into eternity. It is too wonderful – the merest window into lives so far from my own, which, without Solomon's art, I might never have known; never have entered into the communion with them which I am now holding as I gaze. The irresistible allure of ritual – irresistible because it promises to make happen again what can surely only happen once – to perpetuate the moment – to make living and present that which seems to have faded into history – to bring it, living and breathing, within these walls." A gleam from the steadily burning sconces seemed to catch on *Coptic Baptismal Procession*; its gold tints twinkled. "It must be Solomon, and it must be today. Alfred, I require more candles – of deepest red wax – a golden bowl, and a sprig of myrtle."

Stranger and stranger grew his fancy. Counts must be allowed such things, Fred resolved, as their birthright, along with title and lands. They were beginning to conjecture, nowadays, that it was congenital, a madness in the blood. Very prominent veins, the Count had. But surely his blood was as blue as these walls were red; and that still counted for something, a certain deference. Fred would fetch the myrtle and think on the martyr.

In the sepulchral monochrome of the atrium outside the Count's chamber, Fred found himself face to face with Louis; behind him, a stooping figure with a straggling beard, hiding haggard features.

"How is he?" asked Louis.

"Do you mean Stanislaus senior or junior?" Fred brought out with irony.

"He is with his son, then?"

"You persist in calling the thing his son?"

Louis leaned forward so that their visitor might not hear. "It is a strange fancy of his, I admit – to order his doll baptised – I am not sure any priest would assent –"

"He doesn't want a priest. He's going to do it himself. With *him*."

Almost imperceptibly, Louis's eyes widened. "Very well. We must indulge."

"I am sent to find red candles, a golden bowl, and a sprig of myrtle. Do you not think this is another of his – frenzies –?"

"And have we not indulged those before?" Louis's hand was on the brass door handle. "Besides, I am sure the red candles are meant as a complement to the shade of silk shirt he has selected for the occasion. Sir," he addressed the guest, "if you will follow me."

Into the chamber they entered, finding Stenbock in a pose of careful consideration, genuflecting before the marble altar which lay in front of the fireplace. With one hand, he made the sign of the cross;

with the other, he held Stanislaus upright, his head lolling in a fortunate attitude of reverence.

"Sir, I have brought Mr Solomon, as you requested."

Stenbock's head whirled round; in one swift motion, he swept Stanislaus into his arms – limbs flailing – and crossed the room, crying: "My dear Simeon! How long it has been!"

Solomon took both the Count's hands, enveloping boy and man in an embrace. Joy overcame them. It seemed to leap between them like a sprite. With many stammerings and jubilations, Solomon expressed an aching sentiment of having been uncertain whether he and Stenbock should ever meet again.

"In that place, you know –!"

"Oh, horror!"

"You find me changed –!"

"Not a jot!"

"From our former acquaintance –"

"It is as though minutes, not years, have passed."

They proceeded, hand in hand, to the altar, which was laden with peacock feathers, a bronze statue of Eros, and a primitive-looking lamp such as might have been used by the first Christians in the catacombs beneath Rome. Such, at least, was the Count's fancy.

"You keep it always lit?" asked Solomon.

"Always," Stenbock answered. Then a frown overspread his face. "I was once visited by an uncouth fellow by the name of Wilde, who, as I thought, delighted in the beautiful and the curious just as I do. Imagine my surprise when, having momentarily left him to his own devices, upon re-entering the room, I found him lighting a cigarette from this very sacred flame! Too, too shocking – I quite fainted away at the sight – and Louis here tells me that, while I swooned, the odious man positively stamped out the cigarette with his foot, right beside my paroxysm-suffering form. I tell you – there, look – my carpet has never been quite the same."

Solomon peered sadly at the small, singed circle. "And yet the man has been such a passionate advocate of my work," he said. "One would think his cigarette-lighting perhaps akin to passing on a torch."

"Your works, my dear Simeon," with his free hand lightly grazing the back of the painter's threadbare jacket, "will live forever, with or without the intervention of that jackanapes Wilde."

"I am touched by your kind appraisal. They tell me I am beginning to become old; I begin to taste the sere; I despair of how I may be remembered."

With a firmer clasp on the painter's back: "Our progeny has been our art: there can be no greater blessing. My other blessing, indeed, has been the Petit Comte – no – perhaps he is, as Jonson says, my best piece of poetry."

Solomon laid a hand on Stanislaus's head. If he felt, as Louis discerned by a look, that the texture of the hair on the porcelain head was somewhat like that of weeks-old straw, he betrayed nothing, said nothing.

"He is to be baptised today," Stenbock announced with vigour, "by you and me."

"I see that – it must be today," Solomon murmured.

"There is no time to lose. You see what a perilous state of health he is in."

"A font – candles –?" Solomon's hand made gentle passes over the ailing head.

"Alfred is fetching them, with a sprig of myrtle."

"And the oils –"

"Indeed – they must be –"

"Purple."

"Gold."

There had never been any stopping the Count when he took a fancy into his head. Louis braced himself for an instruction of the usual peculiarity; it could hardly be queerer than when Stenbock had sent him off in search of flowers freshly laid on a well-attended grave, or asked him to melt down the statue of Psyche which had once accompanied Eros, and fashion the remnants of it into gold paint.

"Louis, you must bring us two bottles of oil paints for the baptism – one purple, one gold. Simeon, do join me in a drop – just a drop – of red wine, in celebration of the baptism of our son…"

So Psyche had reared her head –! Louis could little fathom this latest intention, but he duly excused himself from the room. He and Fred met again in the atrium, the latter encumbered, arms full with candles, a wide basin of dull gold, and, its flowers softly white and pompom-like, a sprig of myrtle.

"He has requested – paints..."

"Is Mr Solomon to make a painting?"

"For the baptism..."

An eyebrow shot up; a second eyebrow shot up. "He cannot mean –?"

"To besmirch the thing by spattering it with paint? Your guess, as goes the English saying, is as good as mine."

"Do you feel, perhaps, that we are colluding – aiding – abetting –?"

Louis's face remained blank. "It is no crime, as far as I am aware, to baptise a doll in paints. It is simply bizarre."

"Unnatural, I call it. And maybe heresy."

"Our master will have his ways," said Louis with a shrug.

Within five minutes, the scene was set. Only an unsympathetic observer could have found anything amiss in the assemblage: the candles blazing, mounted at various heights; the Indian shawls, the velvet drapes, the peacock feathers, all seeming to broil visibly with anticipation; the couple, one pale, one flushed, stooping over a golden bowl, the boy held lovingly over it. With a series of light, delicate flourishes, Solomon dipped the myrtle sprig into the two glass bottles, first the purple – flick – then the gold – flick – sprinkling the paint over Stanislaus's head.

Cradling his son, Stenbock felt a sudden inclination and began to recite:

Go thou to Rome – at once the Paradise,

The grave, the city, and the wilderness...

With a similar onset of sudden inclination, Solomon, continuing the ablutions, made a rejoinder in hushed tones: "Here lies one whose name was writ in water..."

It struck Louis and Fred, their backs against the door, as somehow apt; they watched as the paint flowed easily, like water, off the doll's porcelain skin. Purple and gold, alike, rushed off him in a river, forming a shallow pool in the golden basin.

Passing a hand crosswise over the face of the Petit Comte, Stenbock went on with his oration:

Peace, peace! he is not dead, he doth not sleep

He hath awakened from the dream of life

'Tis we, who lost in stormy visions, keep

With phantoms an unprofitable strife,

And in mad trance, strike with our spirit's knife

Invulnerable nothings. – We decay

Like corpses in a charnel; fear and grief

Convulse and consume us day by day,

And cold hopes swarm like worms within our living clay.

He looked to be at the point of collapsing onto the cold marble at the foot of the altar, Fred thought with some alarm; in danger of knocking the icon of Buddha into the fire, or of bruising his head against the strong bust of Shelley. But no: the three figures at the altar fell into a tight embrace, before Stenbock lifted his son onto the bed and resumed his maiden-like pose, splayed across the blankets, pressing the boy against him, watching the warmth slowly stealing into his face.

"Look, Simeon," he whispered.

A transfiguration was taking place in the Petit Comte. The deathly pallor had been banished, giving way to a blush, a lightening of the features. His once drooping mouth began to turn upwards; the smile tugged at his cheeks and the corners of his eyes. His eyelids lifted, their bruise-like shades peeling away to give full, shining view of the pupils, two golden dots dancing like dwarf stars; they looked up at the Count and the painter in wonder.

THE MERIT OF A CURSE
by Catherine Yeates

Virgil set his suitcase by the front door and surveyed his new home through its thick layer of cobwebs and dust. An ornate mirror hung in the entryway, and he plucked a handkerchief from his pocket to wipe it clean. He was greeted by a distorted reflection that made his ears, which were admittedly prominent already, appear twice their size. He flicked his fingers over the amateurish spell sustaining the illusion. It broke easily, and Virgil sighed.

His new home cried out for a thorough cleaning, but there was one task of even higher priority: breaking the curses on the furniture his grandfather had left behind.

Below the mirror sat a long wooden table—why someone would curse it to grow moss, he couldn't fathom. With the years, the house had remained empty, and the moss had climbed onto the nearby wall. Virgil searched for any stray threads of magic he might pull to unravel the spell. After a sharp tug, the sigil disintegrated just as easily as the hex on the mirror had. The moss fell from the wall and table, leaving only a pile of desiccated plant matter. He swept the debris into a ball of wind and ushered it out the front door.

The wooden porch steps creaked as he stepped back into the garden. Late afternoon light illuminated the ivy climbing the gray stone wall surrounding the lawn. Virgil snorted at the profanities scrawled out in loops of vines—certainly the work of intrepid young mages trespassing on the property. He dissolved the mess of spellwork on the vines, then pulled a thick stack of letters from his coat pocket.

Virgil's grandfather had made his living breaking hexes, and he had been good at it. After he died, most of his belongings were sold or divvied up among family members. No one wanted to disturb an old hex breaker's collection of cursed objects, so they remained with the house. Virgil couldn't understand why his grandfather had kept them; so far, the spellwork wasn't even worth a second glance. Still, his grandfather had relegated one cursed item to the cellar and left a letter warning any future occupants about it.

Perhaps that one would pose a challenge.

Stale air rushed out as he wrenched open the cellar door. At the bottom of the steps, there sat a large wooden chest with a rounded lid. It was simple yet sturdy, with a dark metal clasp and leather straps.

Virgil scanned the letter. His grandfather had admired the spellwork on the chest and made no move to break its curse. "The curse will only take effect if one attempts to remove it or destroy the vessel," he read. He heaved open the lid.

Mushrooms of all shapes and sizes filled the chest, growing from every inch of the wood. A few slimy caps brushed Virgil's fingers, and he grimaced as the mass of fungus glistened and rippled in the dim light. He scoffed. The spellwork was old and tattered. He would have no trouble removing it.

* * *

Virgil woke the next morning with determination surging through him. He rose from his makeshift bed, a pile of blankets arranged on the floor of the otherwise empty bedroom; the rest of his belongings had yet to arrive. He readied himself for a trip into town. As he strode down the porch steps, he spotted a man staring at his home from the street. The man had a somewhat stocky build with rosy skin and blond hair tinged with gray around his temples. He wore brown slacks and a dark tweed vest over his shirt.

"Good morning," Virgil said stiffly.

"Ah, hello," the man said, smiling, his eyes twinkling in the early light. He was handsome, with a professorial air. "I didn't know anyone lived here. I'm Albion. Dr. Albion Dupont."

"You're a doctor, are you?"

"I used to be an academic. I taught at the mage college to the north."

Virgil relaxed. "Then we have something in common. I'm Dr. Virgil Main. I recently retired from the college the next town over."

"Main, you said? Then you must be related to the man who used to live here. I didn't know him, but I heard he was renowned for breaking curses."

Virgil nodded. "He was my grandfather. Though for all his expertise, he left behind an array of cursed objects in the house when he died. Seems he became eccentric in his old age."

"Indeed? Well, there's that saying. The best hex breakers know when to leave a hex well enough alone."

Virgil wrinkled his nose. "I'd prefer not to have his menagerie hanging around my new home. Call it a bit of a retirement project."

"Best of luck," Albion said. "Please take my card. It has my sigil if you'd like to contact me, or feel free to drop by."

Virgil nodded and waved as Albion left. This town was charming, with cobblestone streets and rows of houses inlaid with intricate woodwork. Ivy grew over brick walls, and flowers filled wood planters. As he climbed the hill to the shopping district, a carriage passed him, the horses shaking their heads as they trotted by. A two-hour carriage ride would deliver him to the nearby college town. It was close enough that he could keep up with news and far enough away that his early retirement was unlikely to be disturbed.

He returned home with cleaning solutions and reagents for spellwork, as well as a few enchanted mops for the dusty floors. In the cellar, he mixed oils and herbs and applied them in a large circle around the wooden chest—a protective spell. Then he dipped a pen into a dark purple elixir and drew sigils on parchment. The parchment plastered itself to the lid of the wooden chest, and as magic buzzed in the air, he nodded with satisfaction.

* * *

The following day, Virgil surveyed the ground floor of the house. It finally smelled clean and fit for habitation. He checked the cellar next. The protective spell on the chest remained intact, and he lifted the lid. The interior was devoid of mushrooms. Virgil smiled and let the lid drop with a resounding clack. He jogged up the cellar stairs, energized and ready to break another hex before lunch. He stretched his hands above his head and idly scratched an itch near his temple, where his fingers caught on something soft and rubbery. Pursing his lips, he headed for the nearest mirror.

Mushrooms protruded from his head. They grew in small clusters, poking out between strands of his gray hair. He plucked them off, and after a moment, they disintegrated into a fine dust. They grew back immediately. He grunted in irritation; the curse was obviously better crafted than he initially thought. He ran through a dozen hex-breaking spells and healing spells, checking each one off his list when it failed. Then he traced a circle in the air and drew the sigil from Albion's card. The circle pulsed with light, and Albion's face appeared within it.

He smiled, eyes bright. "Good afternoon, Virgil. I'm happy to hear from you."

"Yes, of course," Virgil said, stumbling on his words. Albion's smile was brilliant, and Virgil hadn't been prepared for the warmth he felt for it. "I was wondering, where do you buy your reagents for spellwork? Most of my elixirs are packed away."

Albion rubbed his chin. "I'm partial to foraging in the woods for mine. It may help if you told me what you're looking for." Then his eyes flicked between Virgil's face and the mushrooms protruding from his head. "Ah, trouble with a curse?"

"Yes," he conceded. "I found a cursed chest in the basement, and the spell appears to have transferred to me."

"Yes, I see. I had a similar thing happen a few years back. Tried to remove a tricky curse from an otherwise lovely set of paintbrushes. Cursed myself, of course; the hex seems to attract paint to the front of any button-down shirt I wear."

Virgil eyed him. "I'm not sure if you're being serious."

Albion gestured at the patterned vest he wore. "Oh, I'm not making this up. I've taken to wearing vests!"

"Well, they look handsome on you, no matter the reason you wear them," Virgil said with a laugh.

"Thank you. Your own curse doesn't look too terrible. Just cosmetic, isn't it?"

"Presumably, but I'd prefer to remove it soon."

Albion nodded. "I understand. What if I took you to my favorite healer?"

* * *

Albion escorted Virgil to a neat brick house on the other side of town. The front door opened into a tidy room with pleasant, yellow walls and an astringent scent in the air. The healer peered at them over the counter.

"Yes?"

"I'm Dr. Virgil Main. I was hoping for advice about a curse."

"I knew your grandfather. He was good at his craft," the healer said. She drew sigils in the air over Virgil's head and then nodded, her gaze contemplative. "This looks like the work of the Witch."

"The Witch?"

"A sorceress of some fame used to live up on the hill to the north. She was skilled with curses and enchantments—she's been dead for years."

"If she's dead, then why is her curse still working?"

"She was a powerful witch."

Virgil frowned. "Is the curse dangerous?"

"Oh, it's cosmetic. The, hmm, *growths* lack the physiology of real fungi, and they will not produce spores. From my experience with similar curses, you may be prone to flares during times of stress."

"Are you saying there's no way to break it?"

She shook her head. "I'd say it isn't worth the effort. This curse was designed to resist being broken, and it may fade over time. I would suggest reducing your stress levels to see if the symptoms diminish."

"I see," he said, his face falling. "Thank you for your help."

The door creaked shut as Albion followed him outside, worry evident in his creased brow. "Are you alright?"

Virgil's eyelid twitched, and he crossed his arms. "To be told some local witch was so powerful that her curse is practically unbreakable? Preposterous."

"I understand your frustration, but the Witch was notorious for complex spellwork," Albion said. "I'm happy to help in any way I can."

Virgil sighed. "Of course."

* * *

The following week, a carriage arrived with the rest of Virgil's belongings and mistakenly delivered them to a similar address on the other side of town. The stress had tiny blue mushrooms sprouting from his head. He plucked them off in disgust, knowing they would only grow back. Unable to relax, he walked to the address on Albion's card.

"Hello there, Virgil," Albion said, holding the door for him.

His home was bright and cozy, with wood floors and shelves filled with books and knick-knacks. The walls were packed with art, and Virgil spotted collections of paints and a wooden easel with a blank canvas. Albion guided him to the living area, where they sat at opposite ends of the couch.

He gestured, and a teapot and two mugs floated into the room. "Tea?"

Virgil poured himself a cup. "I'm interested in hearing what you know about this Witch."

"I'm no expert," he said. "She passed away decades before I moved here, but she was well-respected—renowned for her potent spellwork. Some people say she learned her craft from a sorcerer in the faerie lands in the north. I heard she was on good terms with the townsfolk, as well as the forest and lake spirits. She was quick to judge those she viewed as misusing natural resources." Albion sipped his tea and hesitated. "We could visit the remnants of her castle. I collect flowers in that area to make paint."

"Excellent," Virgil said, rubbing his hands together.

They set off, hiking over the rolling hills north of town. The grass was green and tall, and it swayed in the warm breeze. The wind ruffled Albion's hair as well, leaving it sticking up, and Virgil briefly considered smoothing it back down for him.

The Witch's castle was a sprawling structure atop the tallest hill, overlooking the town, forest, and distant lake. The towers and adjoining parapets had fallen, now lying covered in moss.

Virgil and Albion walked beneath an elaborate arch into the main atrium, where tattered banners and tapestries hung from the walls. The floor was dusty and dotted with gray bricks that had tumbled from the upper levels, and the rooms that hadn't collapsed held little but broken pottery and wood splinters. At the top of an enormous staircase was a portrait of the Witch.

Virgil's gaze flicked from her sharp gray eyes to her long black hair. "She was striking. And vain enough to ensure at least some of her spellwork survived long beyond her."

Albion nodded. "Indeed."

The second-level hallways led only to the broken towers, leaving little else to see. Virgil sat on the stone fence outside while Albion crouched in the grass, picking the purple flowers dotting the hill and valleys below.

"What flowers are those?" Virgil asked.

"Some people call them witches' hats. Supposedly, they only started growing here after the Witch built her castle."

Virgil snorted and extended his hands, feeling the magic carried by the wind. It hummed in the air, traveling deep into the ground of the hill. He traced the edges of the spells and heard their whispered words, the layers of interlocking incantations encouraging the plants to grow tall and strong. Virgil let out a soft puff of breath. "It seems this Witch was quite a powerful spellcaster."

"You feel it, then. The spellwork that runs through this entire hill and valley," Albion said.

"It's impressive, but if she was capable of this level of magic, why bother with petty curses?"

"I couldn't tell you. Maybe she didn't consider her work petty, as you say."

"It feels petty to me," Virgil said, "but you might be right. Maybe if I can understand why she cast the spell on that blasted chest to begin with, I'll be able to break it."

* * *

His grandfather had provided no other information about the cursed chest, so Virgil turned to the library, where he pored over newspapers. He discovered news articles detailing a major fire that had swept through the valley and forest during his grandfather's era. On his third day of research, he ran into Albion, who convinced him to have lunch at the café down the street. The other man frequently occupied the library as well, sketching from books with diagrams of flowers. Later, he caught Albion softly snoring, a book on paint pigments lying open on the table in front of him.

It was horribly endearing.

After a week and a half in the library, Virgil found what he was looking for. He ushered Albion over to his desk, which was piled full of newspapers and books.

"The Witch helped the town and land recover after a fire," Virgil said. "She grew fond of a garden she tended in the woods. Then a carpenter cut down a tree from the Witch's garden without asking her. She cursed the wood, rendering any object made from it unusable. Frustrated, the carpenter contacted my grandfather and asked him to break the curse."

Virgil picked up another newspaper. "My grandfather refused to do so, instead buying the chest from the carpenter on the condition that he apologize to the Witch. He did, and my grandfather kept the chest afterward."

Albion watched him intently. "An intriguing story."

"I agree. Are there any collections of cursed objects in this town? It seems the carpenter crafted other items from the wood, and I'd like to see what else remains."

"I believe the historical society has an archive of such things," Albion said.

"Excellent, I'll head there now if you'd like to accompany me."

They walked across town only to find the historical society closed for the day. Virgil pinched the bridge of his nose and swallowed his irritation. "Just when I was finally making progress."

Albion patted his shoulder, leading him away from the darkened windows he kept peering into. "I understand you are keen to solve this mystery, but please don't stress yourself. We can come back tomorrow."

* * *

The next morning, the knocking at his door was polite but persistent.

"Virgil, I know you're in there. I saw you through the window," Albion called. "Listen, it's fine if your plans changed—I only wanted to check on you."

Virgil opened the door and ushered Albion inside. "Alright, come in quickly."

"What is that you're wearing?"

He pulled the hood tighter against his head. "My cloak."

"Indoors?"

"I'm having another incident. I do not wish to look at them," Virgil said, his hands clenched.

Albion tilted his head at him. "Is this outbreak bothersome?"

"They're all bothersome."

"I thought you weren't bothered by the last batch. You didn't cover them when we were at the Witch's castle."

"You *saw* those?"

Albion raised an eyebrow. "The small blue ones? I daresay they were almost cute."

Virgil scowled and lowered his hood. "These are grotesque." Clusters of ruffled brown mushrooms grew in a ring around his head. They overlapped each other, forming a mass of curling fungi that swayed as he moved.

"Ah, hen of the woods," Albion said. "I don't find them grotesque, but they are noticeable. Did something trigger them?"

"Stress and frustration." Virgil took a long sip from his mug. "I received a letter from a colleague expressing his regrets that I retired. Naturally, that sent me into a spiral of anxiety, and then these horrific things appeared."

"May I ask why you retired?"

Virgil sighed, leaning back in his seat. "I liked my job at the college, but I took on too much work until I finally exhausted myself. This was meant to be a period of rest for me."

"I understand that," Albion said. "When I left my position, I still thought I might return to academia, but instead I found myself more drawn to the arts."

"I am glad you've found something you enjoy," Virgil said ruefully. "I had hoped to take this time to reevaluate what to do with the rest of my life." He scoffed. "I thought I might take up occasional work as a hex breaker like my grandfather. Foolish of me."

Albion shook his head. "Not foolish."

"But I was a fool to think I could break this curse so easily, and it feels as though now I'm being punished for my hubris."

"For *hubris?*" Albion huffed. "Who among us hasn't tried to break a complex curse as a test of skill, or an experiment, or merely for fun? The outcome would have been the same regardless of your mindset. It is an occupational hazard."

"I suppose you're right," Virgil said. "I ought not to be so unpleasant about it; after all, you went out of your way to come see me."

"I thought we made plans to visit the historical society today. I was concerned when you didn't arrive, and so I came to check on you. Now, I can't avail you of your predicament, but there is one thing I can offer that may help."

"Yes?"

"A hug, if you like."

"Certainly," Virgil sputtered.

Albion stood and stretched out his arms. Face heating, Virgil hugged him. He was warm and smelled like paper and dried flowers.

"You know, crowns of flowers are fashionable among the nature mages. I'm sure some throw in a few mushrooms for good measure," Albion said, rubbing his back.

"I'm an old historian, not a nature mage. Such a crown would look much better on you."

"Well, I've heard that royalty from the faerie lands wear mushrooms in their crowns, if that idea appeals to you more."

Virgil laughed. "That's even more ridiculous." He rested his head on Albion's shoulder for a moment and then pulled back, patting him on the arm. "Thank you, my friend. I appreciate your kindness."

* * *

Books lined the walls of the historical society building. Virgil brushed past the rows of tables as he headed to the second floor. The gallery housed dozens of enchanted objects, many of which were locked behind glass displays. At the far end sat a wooden dresser with leafy branches emerging from its drawers.

"That must be it," Virgil said and approached the sign on the wall, pulling out his reading glasses. "Ah, it's too dark." He traced the first two lines of his light sigil in the air when his wrist tingled. A cluster of small, glowing mushrooms sprouted from his arm, illuminating the words. He grimaced and exchanged a glance with Albion, who looked at him oddly. Virgil turned to the sign.

"Yes, this was the work of the Witch," he said as he read the description. "This dresser was made from the same tree as the chest in my grandfather's basement. The Witch said that her favorite things about the tree were the beautiful leaves and the mushrooms that grew from a dead branch that had fallen to the ground. She called her curse 'an enchantment to bring out the natural beauty of the wood.'"

"This dresser is beautiful in its own way," Albion said. "Either she was being cheeky, or she didn't actually view her spells as curses."

"I don't know what else you call a spell designed to cause someone grief."

"This dresser isn't causing anyone grief anymore." Albion shrugged. "What is the difference between an enchantment and a curse? Little."

"Yes, there is little academic difference between enchantments and curses, but most curses have no functional utility," Virgil said.

Albion rubbed his chin and then gestured to the dresser. "This reminds me of a story I heard about a cursed ring. It was said that anyone who put it on their finger would live only ten more years. The ring was passed down as an odd family heirloom, and a man wore it on a chain around his neck. He'd inherited it from his grandparents, and he found it beautiful."

"Seems dangerous to keep something that powerful around."

"Maybe," Albion said. "But this man was hiking up a steep mountain, and he fell. He was badly injured and losing blood, with no one around to help him, so he put on the ring."

"And?"

"He lived exactly ten more years."

"Did this actually happen?" Virgil asked. "Because it sounds like a parable."

"I can't verify that it's true. But the point is that enchantment is a subjective art. Many enchantments also gain power when they're regularly invoked and may wear off if they aren't invoked. The best option would be to learn what invokes your curse and avoid those things."

Virgil crossed his arms. "I thought you were an artist, not an expert on curses."

Albion's eyes flashed with irritation, and he drew in a long breath. "If you'll recall, I used to be an academic as well. What I do in my retirement from academia does not diminish my knowledge from my earlier career." He pointed to the glass display. "Breaking the Witch's enchantments is like taking a house apart brick by brick. Yes, it can be done, but it would take more effort and as much time as letting the curse fade naturally."

"Are you telling me I should wait months or years on the off chance it fades?" Virgil asked.

"I'm saying I agree with the healer and that reducing your stress levels will go a long way. Of course, you must try not to invoke it inadvertently."

"What *exactly* do you mean by that?"

Albion gestured to Virgil's wrist. "You wanted light, and mushrooms appeared. Like it or not, the curse is now tied into your physiology and magic. If you want it to go away, you must avoid invoking it. Or better, stop fixating on it and live your life."

Virgil scowled. "Easy for you to say. You don't have these protuberances popping out of your head. But here they are, a testament to my ineptitude at magic."

"For goodness' sake, you don't need to treat a silly spell as a punishment. You're making it mean all sorts of things it doesn't need to mean."

"It means that with all my years of experience as an academic mage, I was outdone by some local witch," Virgil snapped.

Albion's eyes narrowed. "You don't even care about the curse itself, do you? You're sore because you don't see the Witch as a proper scholar. Academic snobbery is what that is." He crossed his arms, turning away from Virgil. "This is the sort of nonsense I left academia to escape."

"Well, I guess it's unfortunate that I moved to your town," Virgil said. He opened his mouth again and shut it. "I'm leaving before I say something else I regret."

* * *

Virgil spent the next days sulking about the house. Spindly coral fungi had sprouted from his head overnight, but his malaise had more to do with how he had treated Albion. The man had seen his wounded pride.

Virgil stared at the ceiling—he needed a change of pace.

He packed a bag and headed into the nearby woods. As he followed the trail, he passed a woman wearing an emerald-green tunic embroidered with gold and a circlet atop her head. She had warm brown skin, pointed ears, and long, braided hair. Virgil wondered if she could be royalty from the faerie lands, judging by her attire, but she only nodded to him and continued walking.

Virgil hiked through the thick woods, past gnarled trees and slow-flowing streams. Just when he considered resting, the trail opened into a field with thousands of flowers of every hue imaginable. They were beautiful and bright, and it occurred to him that perhaps Albion could use them to make pigments. Or he might simply appreciate a bouquet and an apology. Virgil glanced around and saw no one, but these woods were wild. He knew enough to be mindful of the forest's denizens.

"Is anyone there? I would like to pick a few flowers if that would be acceptable."

A moment passed, and wood creaked behind him as a dryad emerged from a tall sycamore tree. She nodded to him with a toothy smile. "Someone knows his manners. Very polite. Yes, you may pick flowers, but I would ask for your help."

"What help do you need?" he asked, taking care not to agree to anything without knowing what she wanted.

She led him to an old tree, barren of leaves. "This tree is dead. And yet I've had difficulty convincing the fungi to do their jobs. Maybe you can talk to them."

"I'm afraid my, ah, fungi result from a curse and aren't indicative of any skill with mycology," Virgil said.

The dryad shrugged. "If the mushrooms see friends around, they might get the idea. Do your best."

He nodded and rested his hands on the tree, willing the fungi to grow there. A cluster of oyster mushrooms popped out beneath his fingers, glowing faintly with magic.

The dryad leaned closer. "You're right—those aren't real, but they look nice. Go ahead, pick as many flowers as you would like."

He collected two dozen, but the stems did not fit in his satchel. He wrapped them with his handkerchief and carried them. He considered returning home, but as the trail wound through the woods, nothing looked familiar.

"Are you lost, my friend?" a woman called.

She was the faerie woman from earlier. She sat in a clearing he didn't recall passing, accompanied by a man with tanned skin and black hair. The man's ears were long and pointed as well, studded with many earrings.

"Come, sit with us," he said. "Your flowers are lovely. For three, I'd trade you a small fruit pie."

Virgil sat near him on a low stump covered in mushrooms. He was hungry, after all, and he held the bundle out to the man. "Pick any you like."

The man smiled and selected two deep purple tulips and a daffodil. "Beautiful," he said. "And where are the rest going?"

"To a friend," Virgil said. "I'm afraid I was unkind to him when we last spoke, and I would like to apologize."

The woman laughed. "In that case, take a second pie for him."

The man nodded. "I know my husband will be happy to get these. Hopefully, your friend will as well."

Virgil bit into the pie and tasted sweet, tart berries, buttery crust, and cinnamon. It was delicious. The tension finally left his shoulders as he sat there, laughing and talking. Finally, he worked up the audacity to ask the question in his mind.

"You may have noticed that I have a curse," he said, gesturing at his head. "I was wondering, is it true that members of faerie royalty sometimes wear mushrooms in crowns?"

"Perhaps," the woman said with a smile.

"And perhaps you should start your trip home if you'd like to be back before dark. This forest is safe, but it can be difficult for you humans to see," the man said.

"Thank you for your hospitality," Virgil said, and bowed his head.

He still didn't make it back by dark. After tripping over the third root, he willed the glowing mushrooms to return, and they extended from his hands and head, shining brightly enough to light the path. They illuminated his front door when he finally arrived home.

Virgil examined the small, luminous mushrooms. "I suppose I could find some use for these if I wished." Then he dropped the flowers into a large cup of water and collapsed into bed.

* * *

The next day, Virgil gathered his courage and made his way to Albion's home. The other man stood in his backyard, humming to himself in front of his easel. His yard opened to the fields, and Albion was painting the flower-covered hills and distant forests lit by the morning sun. Then he spotted Virgil and smiled, though a tightness remained around his eyes. "Good morning. What brings you out this way?"

Virgil drew in a deep breath and steadied himself. "I owe you an apology. You have been kind to me, and I have been unpleasant, self-absorbed, and rude. I'm sorry, my friend."

Albion's eyebrows quirked upward, and he set his paintbrush in a cup of water. "I accept your apology. Though I'm afraid I'm also responsible. I've been dismissive of your feelings, and I'm sorry for that."

"You were right that I've been fixating on this curse," Virgil said. "It's also true that I have a tendency for academic snobbery. I'm used to defining myself by my work. I thought if I wasn't an academic, I might be a hex breaker, and I couldn't imagine someone wanting to work with a hex breaker so obviously afflicted by a curse."

"I understand, and I believe you have plenty of time to redefine yourself," Albion said.

"Thank you." He handed Albion the bouquet and fruit pie. "I wanted to offer you a proper apology along with these."

Albion's mouth hung open as he accepted the flowers and examined them. "Virgil, they're lovely. Where did you get them?"

"A dryad's garden. I asked her first, of course. And then I traded some to people from the faerie lands for the pie."

Albion laughed. "It sounds like you've had an interesting day. Thank you, Virgil. Now, let me get them into water."

Virgil held the door for him as Albion bustled into the house, clinking glasses while he began his search for a vase. Virgil smiled and stood out of the way, basking in the warm light spilling in through the open window. Then he spotted a large sketchpad resting on another easel. There was a drawing, a portrait of a man rendered beautifully in pencil. After a moment, Virgil recognized his own face and beard, along with the crown of mushrooms around his head.

"Oh goodness, I didn't realize I'd left this out," Albion said. He folded his hands, swaying where he stood. "I hope it's not too bothersome. The image was striking, and I thought it might be a good subject for a study, but I know it's a sensitive thing for you and I—"

"It's wonderful," Virgil said. "You made me look beautiful."

Albion's cheeks and ears glowed brilliant red. "I only tried to draw what I saw. I thought you looked regal, with a crown about your head like that."

Virgil glanced between him and the drawing, and his own face heated. He opened his mouth, and before he could think, he asked, "Would you come over for dinner tomorrow?"

"Absolutely," Albion said immediately. "If you like, we could visit the market together in the afternoon."

"That sounds lovely," Virgil said and smiled.

* * *

They met at the market the next day. The streets were lined with hundreds of stalls filled to the brim with vegetables, fruits, and colorful, magical potions. The wind ruffled Virgil's hair, stirring the mushrooms that protruded from his head like small antlers near his temples. He didn't bother covering them, seeing as it was busy at the market and there were more interesting things than gray mushrooms in gray hair.

Albion chatted enthusiastically with the owner of a stand selling pigments and paintbrushes while Virgil shopped for carrots, turnips, and fresh herbs. Some delicate culinary mushrooms caught his eye nearby, which made Virgil huff to himself. Albion returned with a large bag full of painting supplies and glanced between him and the fungi.

"Do you like mushrooms in pasta?" Virgil asked.

"I do. I am fond of oyster mushrooms," Albion said.

"As am I, provided they aren't growing from my head." The corner of his mouth quirked up. "It's a good thing you're here, as you can be certain they haven't come from my body."

Albion snorted and patted Virgil's back. "I can be sure of that, regardless. After all, yours disintegrate when removed."

"One small thing to be thankful for."

When they arrived at Virgil's home, they were greeted by a basket sitting on the porch. It smelled of fresh fruit and buttery pastry. Virgil opened the paper covering the top and saw delicately wrapped pies.

"Goodness, that looks like the crest of the faerie lords," Albion said. "Who exactly did you meet in the woods?"

"There was a woman with long braids and a gold circlet. She wore a beautiful green tunic, and I believe it had this crest on it. The man had dark hair, and I think he wore a different crest."

"That may have been Cyathus, the faerie lord, and his sister-in-law. Cyathus comes from the faerie lands to the north, and he married the reigning lord of the faerie lands to the west."

"It was kind of them to send a gift," Virgil said. "And perfect timing, as I forgot to buy dessert."

Albion politely insisted he be allowed to help, and Virgil sent him to gather wood from the pile behind the house and start the fire in the oven. They chopped vegetables to roast and prepared a sauce for the pasta, and soon, savory aromas filled the kitchen. When dinner was ready, they sat at the table in the dining room, which Virgil had draped in a navy cloth.

After the plates were empty and fruit pies devoured, Albion leaned back in his chair with his hands on his stomach and sighed. Virgil brushed the crumbs from his beard and closed his eyes.

"Is that clock right?" Albion asked. "I didn't think it was so late."

"It runs one hour and twenty-eight minutes fast, if my watch is correct."

"A curse?"

"Breaking it would mean dismantling and possibly destroying the entire clock. Didn't seem worth it." He searched Albion's face for a reaction and found only a warm smile. "I have decided to be more judicious about which curses I break. It may serve me better to donate the items I dislike to the historical society instead."

"Indeed," Albion said. Then his eyes widened, and he sat up, reaching for the basket that had held the fruit pies. "There's a note at the bottom." He handed it to Virgil.

Virgil opened the thick paper impressed with a golden crest, and he blushed. "We hope to see you at the midsummer festival this weekend," he read. "Bring a guest and wear your finest crown."

* * *

The hills and fields erupted with brilliant purple flowers as the weekend arrived. The rose gardens bloomed, and flowers of every color spilled from the window baskets in town. Tiny lights glowed in the tree branches, and thousands of fireflies floated through the streets. Lanterns marked a path to a field on the outskirts of the woods, where massive tables and hundreds of chairs appeared.

The night of the festival, Virgil donned his tailcoat over gray trousers and a silver vest. A ring of coral fungi and delicate blue mushrooms formed a crown, with a few oyster mushroom clusters for added drama. With some effort, he convinced them to glow.

"Goodness, you look lovely," Albion said. He wore a brown tweed jacket with leather patches on the elbows, along with a waistcoat and a dark green cravat.

"You look wonderful yourself."

Virgil leaned in and rested his hand on Albion's shoulder, debating whether to press a kiss to his cheek. He hesitated, the moment wearing on until he had to act or he'd be standing here staring at Albion all night. He settled for offering Albion his arm instead.

Albion only laughed and interlocked his arm with Virgil's as they strode down the cobblestone streets. Lanterns lit the field, and the flowers that dotted the grass radiated light of their own. People chattered among themselves, sitting at tables or dancing to string music. A long table was filled with food, from roast pheasants and ducks to every manner of vegetable, to pies, puddings, and tarts. At the far end of the table stood two men in fine clothing, greeting guests with waves and big smiles.

"That's who I met in the woods." Virgil inclined his head toward the man with long, black hair. He wore a shimmering blue tunic embroidered with silver, his head adorned by a crown of silver flowers.

"That is Cyathus," Albion said. "The other man is his husband, Proteus, the lord of the nearby lands." The faerie lord was a tall man with brown skin and a shaved head. He wore an ornate outfit of gold and silver with a crown of golden leaves and flowers that glittered in the darkness.

Steeling himself, Virgil approached the pair and bowed his head. "My lords, I wish to thank you for the lovely gifts and for the invitation."

"Of course," Proteus said. "We welcome you."

Cyathus glanced between Virgil and Albion and smiled. "Please enjoy yourselves. And Virgil?"

"Yes?"

"You wear a beautiful crown."

Virgil stuttered a thank you and ran his fingers through his beard as they walked away. He hazarded a glance back at Cyathus and his long, dark hair, flowing in the summer breeze. "I've been thinking," he said to Albion, "Cyathus reminds me a bit of the Witch."

"I see what you mean," Albion said. "It's been said that Cyathus was born to two powerful mages, and the fae never specify whether one of his parents might have been human." A moment passed, and he squeezed Virgil's arm. "Gosh, would you look at those pies?"

They feasted on crispy pheasants and roasted vegetables before returning for fresh fruit, puddings, and pie. Once stuffed, they wandered over to a lounge area, where colorful pillows lay piled on beautiful rugs. Virgil collapsed onto a stack of long pillows and watched the fireflies float through the woods. Albion rested his head on Virgil's shoulder and sighed.

"I'm happy you're here with me," Virgil said. "I hope we'll continue to spend time together."

"I would like that."

The moon was bright overhead, and fireflies floated at the edge of the field. Gradually, more people took to dancing, and the band played a louder, faster tune.

Virgil gently rested his hand between Albion's shoulders. "Would you come with me?"

Albion grinned and followed him to a large tree just beyond the edge of the woods. "Whatever would you invite me back here for, Virgil?"

"I happen to find the scenery lovely. But not as lovely as you."

"Oh, come here already," Albion said and lightly pushed him against the tree. Then he rested his hands on Virgil's hips and kissed him for a long moment.

"It looks like that tree is occupied," someone said in a loud whisper.

They broke apart, and Virgil peered over Albion's shoulder, spotting the faerie lords near another tree a few feet away. They were holding hands and laughing, and he could have sworn that Cyathus winked at him before they vanished further into the woods. Albion laughed and rested his forehead against Virgil's chest.

* * *

Virgil woke to soft rustling in the blankets beside him. He looked at Albion, from his messy blond hair tinged with gray to the lines under his eyes and around his mouth. The lines deepened as Albion grinned.

Albion's eyes flicked to the crown of mushrooms, still decorating Virgil's head. "I think they glow brighter when you blush," he said. "It's remarkably endearing."

Virgil huffed. "Why am I not surprised by that?"

"So, my dear, do you think you'll keep trying to break this curse?" Albion asked.

"No, I think I'm growing to like my crown."

THE STRANGE TALE OF SIGURD AND RADEGAR

By James C. Clar

Sigurd lived in a land of cold mist and perpetual twilight. His days were spent toiling at his nets as the sea battered the black rocks and grey sand of a narrow shore. At certain times of the year—or when the weather was particularly bleak—the earth, sea, and sky seemed to meld into one colorless mass. Under such conditions, the fugue of light and shadow rendered it particularly treacherous for those who made what passed for a living they could from a sea that all but girdled their forlorn, isolated country.

One particularly dreary day, as Sigurd made his way home with his meager catch, he spotted something unaccountably bright lying on the damp silt just ahead of him. Indeed, the strange object seemed to glitter in the half-light. He picked it up. He was, at first, confused and even a bit frightened.

The oval object, although quite thin, seemed to possess a certain depth, an almost fathomless quality. After a few moments of disorientation, Sigurd understood. He had seen a similar device once before. It had been exhibited by a trader from a distant land passing through many years ago. Many people believed such items were magical. Sigurd smiled, a rarity for him, at the thought of such nonsense. He placed the oval in his pocket. He would surprise his wife with his find after their evening meal.

Later, as Sigurd was washing up after dinner, Radegar noticed a few new holes in her husband's battered and weather-stained coat. Taking the garment down from the hook on the back of their cottage door, she began sewing by the dim, wavering light of a candle. As she finished, she felt something in Sigurd's pocket. Her curiosity got the better of her manners, and she reached in to investigate. As she examined what she had found, she gasped. She then began to sob.

When Sigurd rejoined his wife, he found her crying. In her hands, he noticed the object he had picked up earlier on the shore.

"You've found another woman," Radegar stated plaintively.

Sigurd laughed, even rarer than a smile.

"Nonsense, I have enough trouble feeding one. Besides, that's yourself you are looking at. I believe they call it a 'mirror.' Here, I'll show you." With that, he knelt beside his wife, took her hands gently in his, and began to explain.

As the weeks and months passed, Radegar became increasingly fascinated with the mirror. She'd spend hours, quite literally, staring at her reflection in its cloudy depths. She began to neglect her domestic duties. Sigurd's frustration at his wife's behavior was mixed with genuine concern. He considered the possibility of removing the object secretly from their dwelling and, perhaps, destroying it. He resisted the urge, fearful of Radegar's reaction should she catch him in the act. Besides, he reasoned, what harm was there in her benign captivation?

One late afternoon, Sigurd returned home to find the cottage empty. There was no reason Radegar should not be there waiting for him. She always was. "You work hard," she'd say. "Your wife could do nothing less than greet you when you arrive home."

The fisherman searched his dwelling. He went outside and combed the area around the cottage. He checked with the few neighbors who lived within walking distance. No one had seen Radegar.

As night began to fall, Sigurd went back to his cottage. He was hoping against hope that he'd find Radegar there, safe and sound, with a story about some adventure or other that might explain her earlier absence. The place was still empty.

He lit some candles, and as he did so, he found the mirror that had captivated his wife lying on her chair. Sigurd picked up the device and examined it by the soft glow of the setting sun. There, just beneath his own image, he noticed something else—the milky contours of a face. Heart beating, he spun around. Radegar must have slipped quietly back into the cottage—but he was alone in the room.

From that point on, Sigurd, like his wife before him, became enthralled by the mirror; convinced the shadowy figure he sometimes saw beneath its surface was his beloved Radegar. Perhaps those vague stories he had heard so long ago were true.

The lonely months passed in monotonous profusion. Sigurd spent less and less of his time fishing. All but a few hours of each day now found him staring into the infernal object, silently communing with his lost wife.

The people who lived near Sigurd were, like him, a private and taciturn lot. They kept to themselves, but, in their own way, they looked out for one another. One of his neighbors, after not seeing the fisherman for nearly ten days, decided to investigate. One morning, he knocked on Sigurd's door. When no one answered, he let himself into the cottage. Nothing seemed amiss, but no one was home.

As the neighbor was about to leave, he noticed a small oval object on the kitchen table that seemed to give off its own light. He picked it up in his hands and was startled by his own reflection. He, like Sigurd, had heard about such trinkets but had never actually held one. As he looked intently into what he now recalled was a mirror, he noticed two figures walking arm in arm along a wind-swept shoreline. They smiled and, although he could not be sure, one of them appeared to be waving.

Sigurd's neighbor pocketed the mirror. He hurried home. Puzzled as he was, he was itching to demonstrate its splendor to his family.

A Dress Made of Magic

by Mica Smith

I wish I had more time to tell you this, but Prince Jaspar is setting off on his retreat to the distant Mountain of Myria to "find himself," and he's not bringing me with him. So you have to know now how I came to be a dress made of magic.

* * *

Cormellia's real name was Corma, and she lived in a province on the outskirts of Jaspar's kingdom. It wasn't a particularly poor province, but something about living on the outskirts made her feel poor. When she heard about the royal competition, a casual factoid dropped mid-conversation by a passing traveler, she hurried home from her job at the inn, barely able to contain her excitement.

Her mother and little sister were beside themselves with the romance of the situation.

"A bridal pageant?!"

"How lovely..."

"Well, I think the word they used was 'pageantry,'" Cormellia corrected, checking the tilt of her bronze curls in the mirror. "Something about 'fools in the palace turning the royal line of succession into a game to appease the masses.' But yeah, basically."

"Cormie the *princess*." Her sister's eyes went as wide as the freshly cleaned saucers holding their afternoon tea. "He's definitely gonna choose you!"

"It's Cormellia," Cormellia corrected again.

"Of course, dear," said their mother. "You have our full support if you plan to enter. I believe your sister is right—think about your story! A humble innkeeper's daughter, whose father is dead and gone, her family struggling ever since."

Cormellia lifted her plate to take a bite of puff pastry, taking care not to chip the fine china. "I'd rather Father still be here..."

"He would have wanted it this way. It makes for a beautifully tragic tale of rags-to-riches."

"You're gonna take me to the castle with you, right?" Her sister jumped up and did a mock curtsey while their mother gazed in the middle distance, lost in some memory or fantasy. "I'll be a princess-in-waiting! Take me with you!"

"It doesn't work like that," Cormellia chuckled. Laughing too hard made her chin look weird, she noticed in the mirror. She'd have to do something about that.

The prince had indeed ordered a contest to be held at the palace. He invited women of all backgrounds to present themselves as potential marriage candidates. The details of the contest and how it would be judged were kept from the public, sparking a great deal of speculation: was Jaspar looking for a rare beauty? A good mother to future children? Excellent cooking skills?

When the day of the pageant arrived, a huge crowd gathered before the castle gates, only to be turned away in disappointment by the guards. The prince wished to see each contestant alone in his personal chambers. Cormellia followed a long line of women through a side door into an elegant waiting room, looking straight ahead so as not to mess up her hair.

With this rigid unidirectional gaze, she could only see a few of the other contenders—they were pretty, sure, but they hadn't bothered applying lip powder in a *come-hither* manner nor had they chosen an arrangement of petticoats to set off their curves.

Clearly, they didn't want this like she did.

That thought buoyed her confidence as her name was called. She reviewed everything she knew about the prince as she was escorted upstairs. According to hearsay at the inn, he was a brilliant man who kept to himself. Like all members of the royal family, he was gifted with the magical arts and occasionally performed miracles at public appearances: healing the ill, setting water on fire, divining the future. The prince once foresaw a bloody war that would consume the entire kingdom—and that would only end after a catastrophic event he called an "alien invasion." But that isn't for another hundred years.

Mostly, the prince did what all princes do: lounge in splendor, awaiting his bride.

Cormellia's escort knocked on a grand set of doors. A voice from inside bid that she enter.

The doors swung open, and she saw the prince. He was in a dashing state of undress, with no waistcoat and his shirt untied at the neck. He regarded her with piercing eyes.

"Prince Jaspar," she said in greeting, and dipped low in a curtsey.

"Please, call me Jass."

He stood from where he'd been lounging in a gilded armchair. Crossing to the threshold, he took in her coiffed curls and jeweled earlobes expectantly.

She felt it was her cue to begin. "I am honored to meet you, Jass. I'm eager to demonstrate my talents and special qualities, most befitting of a princess. Though I'm but a humble innkeep's daughter, I can play ballads on the lute and I—"

"What is your greatest desire?"

Her initial annoyance at being interrupted gave way to confusion. "My... what?"

"Your greatest desire." The prince shook his head. "I worded that poorly. If you could wish for anything, right this moment, what would it be?"

This was some sort of test. "I would wish to marry you, my prince."

"No!" She drew back at the shouted word, and he lowered his voice. "I mean something that can't normally happen in this world. Something magical." Was he sweating under his collar?

"I see. Well..." Cormellia looked down at her shoes, then inwardly cursed herself as a lock of hair fell over her eyes, ruining her whole look. She couldn't let this chance slip through her fingers. She had to figure out the correct answer. "Having no gift for magic myself, I've never thought about what magic could give me!"

"I've asked the same question of everyone who's come through my door today. I want you to think of a magic spell. Wish it, and I will make it come true."

"Like a genie," she said dreamily.

"I suppose." The prince's hands hung at his sides as he opened and closed his fists. She couldn't keep him waiting.

Cormellia said the first thing that popped into her head: "I want a dress made of magic."

"A dress," he repeated. "Made of... magic."

"Yes." She wasn't sure if he was incredulous or just confirming her request. "That would be wonderful!"

The prince furrowed his brow. "Do you mean a dress that never gets soiled? That always fits perfectly? Or perhaps a dress that changes style to match your every mood?"

"I just want it to be made of magic," she said, trying to hide her growing uncertainty. Did she sound stupid? After all, she wasn't really sure what magic was.

Jass's hand flew up to his forehead. He massaged his temple in small circles, gazing into space. His nostrils flared as his mind worked.

Slowly, he nodded to himself. His lips pursed, almost smiling. He looked back at her, and she was shocked to see his eyes wide with excitement, like those saucers back home.

"Incredible..." he said. "What a challenge! A dress made of *pure magic*? What does that even mean?" He began to pace about the room, stumbling over his words. "What material is magic made of? Is it a substance or merely an idea? At first, I thought it was impossible. But what if it's not? And I could be the first to discover it!"

Then his excitement simmered to incoherent murmuring, incomprehensible words that she thought might be magic-related. Suddenly, he drew himself up and stopped before her. "I've got it!"

He reached out to grab her arms, and Cormellia recoiled. "What are you doing?" she blurted in spite of herself. Obviously, the prince could do what he pleased, but this *Jass* person was making her uncomfortable.

"I need to take your measurements. To make the dress."

"My... measurements?" She wanted to cover herself up with both hands.

"It's all right," he said with a surprising softness, and ran his fingers down her elbows to the inside of her wrists. She knew he could feel the flabby skin under the artfully aligned folds of her flared silk sleeves. Her hair stood on end.

Jass's hands moved to her waist—disgustingly thick, she had always thought—and her hips, with the bone protruding out like the ribs of a sick dog. She hated her hips.

He traced the outer curve of her thighs, her knees, her calves. He dwelled for a long moment on her ankles. Because they were shapeless and ugly, she was sure.

Finally, he returned upwards to her shoulders, before his hands travelled to her neck.

She was breathless as his fingers lingered there.

"That should do it," Jass said, gently withdrawing his hands. "Now, let's see what I can do."

The prince moved to the center of the room and closed his eyes. Eyelids fluttering, he weaved his fingers through the air, miming the same movements he had made on her body. He repeated the movements over and over. Soon, sparks flew in the wake of his whirling arms, coalescing into sheets of white light. They layered on top of themselves like fabric, settling into a solid shape as if he were sculpting them out of thin air.

When he'd finished, his hands falling to his sides, a dress made of magic floated before her.

Cormellia clapped her hands. "Well done, my prince!" She wasn't quite sure what had happened, but Jass looked completely spent, like he'd just run a hundred-mile footrace.

"Now put it on," he commanded in a faint voice.

"Uh... how?"

Cautiously, she stepped into the dress. A veil of light passed over her eyes, and she felt a strange coolness on her skin. The dress she had been wearing before was wreathed in light, then changed shape.

Cormellia stepped toward a nearby mirror, pulled by primal instinct.

"Oh," she said.

"Well?" Jass said, collapsing onto his chair.

"It's not very flattering."

He stared at her.

"Look," she said, turning, "it makes my butt look big."

"Let me try something." He waved his hands wearily, sparks crackling as he reshaped the dress. The hemline climbed above her waist, ethereal fabric skimming her hips to slim her lower torso.

"Hmm," she said, scrutinizing her reflection again. "That's better, but... what about the edge of this sleeve here? My arms look weirdly long."

"I'll try a different angle..."

* * *

The wedding was held on the palace grounds, with all the grandeur of a royal celebration. The ceremony was attended by thousands from all over the kingdom. Cormellia, who had become known among the people as "the prince's muse," wore her magic dress covered by a traditional white lace veil, for she was embarrassed that the cut of the bodice made her shoulders look like a man's.

Keeping a dress made of pure magic constantly in existence took all of Prince Jaspar's energy. He no longer had time for—or interest in—performing petty miracles. Lines grew prematurely on his forehead, and his face had fallen gaunt. His condition only worsened when his new wife suddenly disappeared on their first anniversary. Distraught with panic, he sent guards to find her. A courier delivered a letter the next day: "I have realized that my flaws do not define who I am. Your love has helped me see that. But now I know what I truly want: to be a musician. I've gone to study with the Guild of Bards... I will not be returning."

The loss of Cormina—she had changed her name again, to fit her new life—filled Jass with a strange new energy, new inspiration.

He no longer has the time to maintain me, the dress made of magic, left hanging in the royal closet.

In fact, he's decided to forget about magic for a while. Once he leaves for his upcoming mountain journey, he'll cease pouring his energy into me, and I'll no longer exist. At least, not as a dress. Perhaps I'll become something else, for someone else. Maybe even you... now that you know my story.

What use I serve next is up to you.

Summer Horse

By Yucheng Tao

I

A horse collapsed in the wild,
no rain, no water in its mouth.
The horse's eyes were fixed on the mountain.
A gray house lingered in my vision behind the horse.
The dry weather gnawed at me,
caught between illusion and truth until I woke.

II

Outside the window, rain had not visited for a year.
The stones paving the streets lay rotten, broken.
In this rainless city, my life felt dull and dry.
But the mountain flashed bright as the horse gazed at it.
The horse might arrive, or it dwells in my dream—
a land of freedom,
a promised land from God.

III

Here, a massive, concrete-gray box was in the city's corners.
Here, I sank into the deep gray.
And everything was gray—
except for the horse in my mind.
Broken bottles echoed with noise from my father,
his face burgundy with rage in the living room.
I folded myself into smaller boxes,
my room's door tightly shut.
Inside my bones, in the space of my dreams,
a horse grew stronger, yearning to flee this circle.
I swiped shards of glass from the floor,
while disappointment lingered like the scorching summer.
For me, it was an ordinary and terrible night.
But the horse never stood waiting at my door—
it never truly arrived to carry me away.

IV

When the long-lost rain finally fell,
I longed even more to leave the suffocating home,
drowned in bottles and drugs.
Between imagination and reality,
my bones grew hard, like the horse.
When I rode it to find my road,
my road would be clear:
No gray. Not dry.

V

When the rain ceased,
I spoke once more of the horse in my dreams:
"It gallops through fields; it gazes on mountains."
My words carried a coolness then,
even as the relentless sun burned outside.
But I said to myself,
neither the summer nor the concrete box
could diminish my courage.
I knew rain, summer horse, mountain—
what they meant to me.
I would leave and run
when I became braver.

THE SENTINEL AND BODHISATTVA
By Charlie Freelander

The Sentinel, 102 AD

The gray waves roiled and crashed to the cliffs far below. The salty wind tousled Quintus Flavius's hair and tugged at his cloak. Quintus crossed his arms and kept his eyes steady on the horizon. He stood watch, and he took his duties seriously.

From down at the bottom level of the watchtower came dragging noises, heavy footsteps, occasional swearing and bursts of laughter. The battle-hardened veterans of the detachment of Legio XX Valeria Victrix were preparing to patrol the boggy forests of Caledonia.

"…standing up there, a stick up his ass. Have you ever seen the man laugh or smile?" a new man said in a gleeful, subdued voice, ignorant of just how keen hearing Quintus had.

Nobody answered. Instead, all activity ceased.

It was Marcus Tullius Verus who broke the tense silence. "Be quiet, cur. You couldn't ask for a better man than Flavius to have your flank." Quintus could imagine how Verus's bushy eyebrows had drawn together.

"Too right," continued Lucius Strabo. "If the man says he will do something, it's as good as done. So what if he doesn't care for whoring and gambling! More for the rest of us!"

They all burst into laughter and continued their preparations, the new man joining the laughter to compensate for his misstep. Having been part of a few skirmishes didn't give him the right to make fun of a veteran who had been there from the start.

Quintus had been a fresh-faced recruit when he marched north against the Brigantes under Agricola. Thus, he refused to remember the new man's name until he proved himself further. Being ridiculed because of his serious, dutiful nature didn't bother him in the least. Especially from the mouth of an untested recruit. He also knew that his comrades would defend his name.

The corners of his mouth curved slightly at the thought of their whoring and gambling—activities that never held much attraction to him. Once or twice, he had sought the company of a prostitute, but the experience felt undignified. A smile, he acknowledged to himself. That's what it was. *I can smile.* A smile born of fondness for the men he had been to Tartarus and back with.

The natural melancholy of the overcast sky and the gray waves had caught on within Quintus' mind. He had held too many dying companions in his arms, trying to grant them peace in their final moments. Yet they died screaming in agony, gurgling bloody bile, crushed, impaled, or trampled to death in their prime.

As he absent-mindedly took out the cloth to polish the bugle that didn't need polishing, it occurred to Quintus, not for the first time, that the Brigantes and the Caledonii had died that way too. Ambushing the Legio on boggy forest trails and attacking ferociously from the craggy hills of the highlands, where Quintus had slogged uphill in full battle armor. A cog in the machine that was the glorious Rome. There was much blood on his hands.

Quintus shrugged. Such was the way of the world. Such was his duty. Rome demanded, and he did his part.

As the patrol departed and the voices of Quintus's companions retreated to the forest trail, the timber of the watchtower swayed and creaked in the wind. Salty water, carried by the wind from the sea, drizzled on Quintus's face. His mind drifted to scenes from his distant youth, sun-caressed fields and olive orchards around Tusculum. There had been a woman—a girl, really, just as he had only been a boy—he had taken walks with, a respectable and intelligent young lady. Quintus remembered her blue eyes and the ribbon in her hair. They had never openly broached the subject, but Tullia knew Quintus would be rewarded with some land in his retirement.

Back then, the idea of domesticity—a peaceful family life—had felt like something that might bring him contentment and pleasure, but in the distant future. Later, Quintus heard that Tullia had married another and gave birth to twins. *It was for the best.* More than twenty years he had spent stationed in chilly forts with his gambling, whoring, and swearing companions. Trampling soggy mud mixed with blood and gore, knowing nothing but coarse manners, ever-present danger, and death.

He would have no idea how to be a husband, how to hold a child in his arms, how to be gentle. Fighting for the glory of Rome molded Quintus into what he was. It occurred to him, and not for the first time, that when he got too old to serve Rome, he would be a very lonely man. *That day is not here yet.*

A *currach,* a canoe built by the Caledonian tribes, glided across Quintus's view from behind a mass of clouds. The oval-shaped vessels, with wooden frames covered by stretched hide, were used by the tribes both for raiding and transporting cargo. This one plowed the waves in a deep draft, sailing slow and determined. This suggested that it was fully loaded with cargo and not trying to hide its course. There were only a few crewmen on the deck, busy steering and handling the sails. A raiding party would have far more men and little else than their weapons with them. The *currach* sailed over the bay and past the watchtower to the mouth of the river, disappearing from the sight of Quintus's watchful eyes.

Quintus yearned for a moment that he could be on patrol with his companions. Even if he kept quiet most of the time, he enjoyed listening to their familiar juvenile banter. He admonished himself for such wishes. A true soldier of Rome did not complain about his duty. Quintus turned his eyes back to the horizon.

* * *

The Highwayman, 102 AD

"It is done." Mabyn wiped away the strands of copper hair whipping against her mouth in the wind. "The gods-cursed Romans sleep in the bog. The *cailleach* took every last one of them." She spat. "May the wind shred their memory. May their house turn to dust. May nothing ever grow on the salted ground where it used to stand. May the pestilence take the rest of them." Her eyes were pale in the soggy, dimming evening.

"Whoa, Mabyn," the highwayman said. "Remind me never to cross you." Privately, he often wondered why Mabyn held such resentment towards the Romans. Sure, they were conquerors and invaders, but that was nothing new. Whether they came from a neighboring tribe, beyond the mighty rivers, or even across the sea—if it wasn't the Romans, it would be someone else.

Once, after too much to drink, he had asked her. Mabyn shrugged and stared at him with those pale, unblinking eyes. "They don't belong here. They are the end of the old ways," she had said. That was all he was going to get out of her.

Mabyn threw her head back laughing. Leaning on the scraggy and damp bark of an alder, she hiked up her skirts and pulled the highwayman to her chest, wrapping her legs around him. "At first, I tried my dumb, big-teated peasant act on them. They were tempted— who wouldn't be?—but duty, patrol, you know. I guess they've been here long enough to know that we can be dangerous. Would have been much simpler to get them drunk and slit their throats. Instead, I had to bewitch them to feed them to the bog. Spell-binding is so thrice-cursed draining..." Mabyn's lipped curled into a wry grin. "Now, Enough talk. Let's fuck."

There was innocent blood on the highwayman's hands. Still, Mabyn's fervor unnerved him—especially knowing that she was capable of bewitching men into losing their wits, their sense of direction. These Romans were not the first men sleeping in the bog. *Doesn't make her quim any less juicy.*

After the deed was done, he licked salt from Mabyn's collarbones. She responded by nibbling his earlobes. A sliver of moon had risen over the bay, but it was barely visible behind the drifting clouds. Mabyn glanced at the flickering torch on the top platform of the watchtower in the distance. It shone on the cliffs overlooking the bay and the firth. "The watchman's still there."

The highwayman shrugged. "The patrol's dead. Once he figures out they aren't coming back, he'll go home to report. I say leave him be. What's he going to do? Blow into his bugle really hard?"

Mabyn nodded and averted her eyes. "Of course. Better get going, then." She smoothed her rumpled skirts, her face shielded behind a cascade of copper curls.

A knot tightened in the highwayman's belly. He remembered the time when Mabyn had been similarly distant, often seeking the company of that blonde-maned wainwright with the laughing blue eyes. When he finally confronted her about it, she was furious.

"I fuck whom I please!" she had told him.

So, he suffered in silence. But in the end, he emerged the winner of Mabyn's affection. For a long while, he had been Mabyn's favorite lover, the two of them partners in crime as well as in love. If he lost her respect, the conspiratorial spark when their eyes met...

"I guess one less Roman polluting our land is a good thing."

That, he hoped, sounded like a thought Mabyn might approve of.

She raised her eyebrows, looking him in the eye.

They knew these hills and the shadows of the trees surrounding the road. However, the treeline ended well before the cliff towering over the bay. The watchtower on top of it.

"He could see us in the torchlight," the highwayman said.

True, the Roman did not expect to be attacked from land—it was a senseless and foolhardy idea, after all. He was keeping watch over the bay and the approaching vessels. But the watchtower was surrounded by nothing but open terrain. Apprehension and the thrill of sport started to dance in the highwayman's gut, vying for domination.

"You know how to approach a quarry undetected," Mabyn said. "Yet... perhaps it would be foolish not to use a touch of magic. I'm not completely depleted yet."

The highwayman smiled as the conspiratorial spark emerged in her eyes. "What do you have in mind?"

* * *

The highwayman and Mabyn observed the watchman's routine for a time. The man spent most of his time scanning the bay and the firth. But then he'd turn around and take a good look at the surrounding landscape. The highwayman had observed watchmen before—not to attack, but to evade. Some seemed bored and lazy, going through the motions but paying little attention to their surroundings.

Not this man.

Even from a distance, the watchman's posture bespoke stalwart vigilance. This Roman took his duty seriously, even when observing an empty landscape from a secure vantage.

Mabyn counted with her fingers. "He keeps track. Probably carries one of those... drip clocks with him."

A Roman she had beguiled had shown her one such gadget, explaining that it could keep track of time—even in total darkness. "When he turns his back to watch the bay again, we'll make for the tower."

They waited in the shadows of the trees, watching the lone sentinel turn his back and return his gaze to the sea. The pair started their silent sprint. The slippery grass didn't make a sound under the highwayman's softly padding feet. Mabyn followed close behind. The waves crashed against the cliffs, the wind howled, and the timber of the watchtower groaned. Even so, moments when the clouds drifted from the crescent of the moon unnerved the highwayman.

Quick, quick, across the cliff, mindful not to slip or stumble. One more step, two, three—and they were in the shadow of the watchtower, safe from the watchman's gaze.

The highwayman waited as Mabyn closed her eyes and concentrated. After a long moment, she opened her eyes and mouthed, "Go."

One, two… He slid to the bottom level of the tower and kept counting. *Ten, eleven…* embers still glowed faintly in a brazier, illuminating the shapes of an empty weapon rack and neatly made cots. *Fifteen, sixteen…* he found what he was looking for. He nimbly ascended the ladder, grateful for the howling wind to cover the noise of creaking rungs. *Twenty-five, twenty-six…* he reached the hatch and waited for a few moments yet. *Thirty! Go!*

The hatch sprang open, and the highwayman leaped on the platform, illuminated by the moon and the flickering torch in a bracket. The watchman turned sharply, drawing his sword. The highwayman was startled by the man's determination and precision. He faltered. But in the same instant, a gull descended and started to savagely claw at the man's face. *Kii-ee! Kii-ee!*

The watchman swatted at the flapping flurry of wings, swearing in Latin, sending afloat a rush of feathers, but the bird just screeched and pecked at his face ever more furiously. Instinctively, the watchman lowered his head to shield himself from the gull. Relief flooded the highwayman's veins. All it took then was a step and a determined thrust at the base of the neck. At the impact, he momentarily registered the legionary's wiry strength. He would have stood no chance against this man in fair combat. . All the same, the watchman went slack and toppled silently to the platform. His grey eyes were already glassy and sightless as the highwayman rolled the body over.

The agitated bird still screeched. *Kii-ee! Kii-ee!*

The highwayman wiped the blood off his dagger and nudged the body with his foot. The watchman was no young man. His face was lined and gaunt, a few strands of gray in his dark hair. *He might have twenty years on me…*

Kii-ee! Kii-ee!

Mabyn soon followed up the ladder. Extendeding her hand to the gull, she kissed the bird's head and it finally calmed, settling on her palm. She sent it away with a smile and a timid wave. The bird, gliding majestically towards the sea, disappeared in the darkness.

Then she turned to regard the highwayman.

"I killed a Roman… A legionary. A real warrior," he said, feeling the fool as the words escaped him.

"So I see." Mabyn's eyes shifted, becoming frigid and ancient. It seemed like the copper-haired, comely witch was now older than the hills and the sea, even as her face looked fresh and young as ever. Her lips curved into an indulgent smile, a stark contrast to the chill radiating from those ancient eyes. "Well done. Good dog. Come here for your treat."

And the highwayman did, and the quim was still juicy, but something inside of him was cold, so very cold—and the pride he had expected did not come.

* * *

The Vicar, 1758

The mournful bugle had again awakened the vicar. On moonlit nights, a ghost lit eerie beacons and sounded his haunting call. Thus it had been for centuries, as the town had grown sprawling around the remains of an ancient Roman garrison. Most of the old watchtowers along the coast had been dismantled or crumbled to dust. But the remains of the one where the ghost held his eternal vigil over the bay still stood, perched upon the cliff at the river's mouth.

People acclimate to most things. Those who settled on the outskirts near the coal mines at first grumbled about the clatter of the carts, the din of picks, and the occasional explosion disturbing their sleep. But soon enough, it all faded into the background, and they again slept soundly as ever.

The Roman ghost's nightly bugle calls certainly didn't stir most townsfolk from their slumber. Why, then, did the sound trouble the vicar so deeply? Why was it that he startled awake, his heart heavy with a restive melancholy that lingered for days—a pain he could neither name nor soothe?

Pondering that in his sleep-deprived mind, the vicar pushed the door to the Shipwright's Arms ajar. He paused to observe what kind of mood he would be walking into. The chatter was lively, but there were also many frowning faces gathered around Douglas Reardon's table, a wealthy landowner and industrialist responsible for much of the town's recent development.

"Quick, quick, Father, it's chilly outside!" chided Tom the innkeeper. Tom spent his youth at sea and retired when he had saved enough to buy an inn.

The vicar pushed the door shut and headed for the bar. "You were a seaman, Tom. Surely a little bit of chill shouldn't faze you too much," he said, smiling.

Tom grinned and started to draw a tankard for the vicar. "Oh, I've struggled up a frozen rigging and slept with my teeth chattering as icy bilge sloshed about, and everything was damp and never dried. Don't mean I *liked* it."

"A fair point," the vicar said, then thanked the innkeep for the tankard and approached Reardon's table.

"Have a seat, Father," Reardon said, pulling out a chair. Bright green eyes, which missed nothing, scrutinized the newcomer. "We were just discussing the Roman ghost. Something must be done about him." Reardon paused with the air of a man accustomed to being listened to. There was no need to raise his voice, as there would be no opposition.

"He ain't bad for business," Tom remarked from behind the bar, wiping a few drops of spilled ale with a rag. "Some folks travel here just to see him and stay overnight—curious folks with too much money and time on their hands, anyhow. Legends travel, as well as men."

Reardon shook his head. "I understand, Tom, but there is much bigger business at stake. Between the expansions of the port and increase in coal exports, the town is on the verge of unprecedented prosperity. Unprecedented!

"The ghost has been a quaint, harmless legend for ages—charming really—a remnant of our long history." It had been Reardon himself who funded efforts to preserve Roman history in the town. There was even a museum named after him. "But now he confuses ships sailing for the port. They mistake his beacons and bugle calls for a lighthouse or a foghorn."

The shipwright, William Hardwick, crossed his bulky arms and nodded. "Mister Reardon is right. So far, no souls have been lost, but when the North Star was driven to the rocks, it was only by the good Lord's grace that it remained so. Cargo was lost, sure, but the real loss was the irreparable damage to such a beautiful ship."

A sailor who had been rescued from the wreck of the North Star sucked at his pipe and puffed out smoke. "Only a matter of time... I was there. The ghost will kill, sooner or later. Why is it so vengeful?"

Reardon frowned and blew out a long breath. The vicar could see what worried the industrialist. If such sentiment spread among sailors, the shipping magnates would have difficulty recruiting men to crew ships bound for the new port he had invested so much into.

"I don't..." started Ethel Thwaite, the widow of the late parish clerk. She hesitated, tucking a lock of gray hair inside her black bonnet. The men started to chatter, each offering their opinions, but Reardon silenced them by raising his hand.

"Yes, Ethel?" Reardon said. "You had something to say. Let's hear it."

"It is... I don't... I don't think he is vengeful," said Mistress Thwaite. The death of her beloved husband had been very hard for her. Even before that, she had been one of the few townspeople most interested in Reardon's efforts to preserve Roman history. Afterward, she found some measure of solace by borrowing his books and frequenting the museum. She looked up, and her earnest blue eyes met Reardon's. "He is a sentinel, isn't he? The Romans sent soldiers to patrol from the garrison, didn't they? He kept watch for raider ships. The poor soul has kept sounding that bugle for centuries. For whatever reason, he doesn't know that Rome has fallen, and that his watch is over." She dabbed her cheek with a kerchief. "Probably has never heard of Christ and his infinite mercy."

The vicar was struck by Mistress Thwaite's words. What she said was logical, yes—but it was the instinctive spark of recognition of a higher truth that startled him. While the others had perceived the ghost as an obstacle or object of exploitation, Mistress Thwaite understood he was a suffering soul.

He now recognized the feeling that was troubling him. It was compassion. Compassion not as a mere sentiment but rather an intense urge to relieve suffering.

The men gathered around Reardon's table nodded at the widow's words, their faces solemn.

"That makes sense," Reardon said. "But the fact remains that he must be... convinced to leave. Somehow."

Harry Smithson, a sailor, drew a breath. "The papists have special priests that deal with possessions and such."

"What superstitious rubbish!" snapped Mister Langley, the doctor. His white eyebrows drew together as he pierced Smithson with his disapproving gaze. "Papists, indeed!"

Smithson flinched. "It's just—I've sailed with some papists from across the sea. They ain't bad people." He shrugged and studied the floorboards. "I'm just saying."

Everyone looked at Reardon. *Not at me, though I am technically the spiritual authority here*, the vicar thought with wry amusement. As for Reardon, the man fingered his ginger sideburns and thoughtfully cocked his head, opting to stay silent. Although Reardon was as devout an Anglican as anyone, his ancestors hailed from Ireland.

But Reardon remained silent. The vicar braced himself. "No papist magic or ritualism is needed. This is clearly a matter of the spirit," he said with more conviction than he felt. Though he knew the townspeople respected his cloth and position, they only saw him as a young man barely out of the seminar. He could not afford to appear hesitant. "And, at any rate, what the exorcists deal with are daemons— hellbeings that have possessed living people. If Mistress Thwaite is correct—and I believe that she is—this is a lost soul unable to move on. A suffering being. I will go, and I will speak to the ghost."

The crowd gasped.

"Much appreciated, father," said Reardon.

Tom, for once sincere, stared in awe.

Ethel Thwaite clasped the vicar's hands and smiled. "God bless you, Father. I've long felt so sad for the poor thing. Now that my dear Harold has passed, I often wake up at night to his melody."

The vicar smiled fondly at her. It seemed that not everyone slept soundly when the ghost called, after all.

* * *

The cart clattered to a halt, the bumpy journey through the windswept fields over. The ancient forests that had stood in Roman times had been logged long ago.

"This is as far as I'm going, Father," said the shipwright as he offered his calloused hand to help the vicar out of his cart. "It may be that the ghost means no harm, but harm he does, and I'm a simple man used to simple work."

"I appreciate that you took the time to drive me," the vicar said as salty wind whipped his boyish brown locks.

"Least I could do for a man of the cloth," Hardwick answered, patting his mare's cheek and covering her steaming back with a blanket. "I will pray. Who knows what it will take to banish the ghost—the good book is silent on such matters. Godspeed, Father!"

The vicar began his ascent up the windy cliff. Now and then, curious travelers or lads from the town approached the tower when the ghost stood his vigil; But nobody dared to climb it nor attempt speaking with it. All reports agreed: the ghost was a gray, translucent shape of a tall, gaunt man dressed in a legionary's armor like the specimen preserved in Reardon's museum.

As the vicar pulled himself onto the balcony, he saw the apparition for the first time.

There the sentinel stood, arms crossed and transparent in the light of the rising moon as he looked over the bay. The southern corner of the tower had partially crumbled. Only rotted, weathered fragments remained of the wooden rails lining the platform.

The vicar lifted his lantern and peered in the darkness at the tower's foundation, now just a gaping hole. He examined the crumbling corner. The stone was damp and slippery. Moss grew in patches above the masonry. What remained of the mortar crumbled to dust when he touched it. There was no foothold to be had here. He edged closer to the edge of the cliff, placing every step carefully.

The ghost turned to him. "Who goes?"

The vicar felt the words more than he heard them. He could see the ghost's lips moving, but the words reverberated in the back of his head.

"I have come to release you. To set you free," the vicar said, lifting his lantern.

The ghost frowned. "By what authority would you release me from my watch, strange man?"

"By the authority of Christ."

No spark of recognition emerged in the ghost's eyes.

The vicar held the cross at his neck to the light. "Christ in his infinite mercy offers eternal rest for the weary, in a place beyond this vale of sorrow, in which you are trapped."

The ghost's frown persisted. "I know not of this 'Christ.' My duty is to Rome."

The first chilly drizzle of rain rolled down the vicar's forehead, dripping into his eyes. "The gods of Rome were but shadows. There is but one almighty God who rules all."

The ghost uttered a dry laugh. "What manner of almighty god is that, ruling all by himself? Surely a god who commands other gods is mightier. And what of this 'Christ?'"

Despite the chill, sweat poured down the vicar's neck. Ethel Thwaite's compassion had sparked a recognition of his own. Compassion had spurred him to pursue action in a determined manner, lest he lose his nerve. But apparently, he hadn't quite thought this confrontation through. He searched for the words of sermons and prayer books to explain the mercy always warming his heart. The mercy he sought to share, that drove him to become a priest. "Christ *is* God, who became incarnate as the Son. He gave his life so that all would be free of the grip of death."

The ghost's frown deepened as he peered down from the platform. "You babble nonsense. And what talisman do you wear around your neck? Do I see correctly?"

The cross! Only papists believed that the cross on his neck, in and of itself, carried any magical powers. But it was a potent symbol of what he was trying to explain. "The cross is the symbol of Christ's ultimate sacrifice and the salvation it offers to all. You may enjoy it, too, my friend."

The ghost's nostrils flared, the voice growing scornful. "Deserters and the worst kind of criminals hang upon crosses. No glory lies there. What *kind* of gods talk you to me of, proudly displaying an instrument of shame? What is your meaning in distracting me from my duty?"

The vicar lowered the cross. Clearly, theology wasn't getting him anywhere. But the echoes of suffering were as clear as ever, even if the sentinel's stoic facade betrayed none of that.

"I… I know you are weary. I have felt it on sleepless nights when you sound your bugle. You deserve freedom, my friend," he whispered.

The ghost's eyes softened. "I am weary. True," he said, the anger and scorn gone. "It has been long." Then the corners of his mouth tightened. "Regardless, I have duty, little man who talks of strange gods. You are no soldier of Rome, so perhaps you know not what duty means."

"But the empire you serve has long since fallen! Your vigil no longer serves a purpose!"

The ghost was quiet for a moment, frowning, chewing his lip. Then he crossed his arms and turned his eyes back to the bay. "Dust or not, I have my duty. Perhaps this is some peculiar act of kindness of a madman. Perhaps a trick by malign spirits to urge me to abandon my post. That will not be the legacy of Quintus Flavius. Go now, little man, and disturb me no longer."

"But… Christ offers rest and mercy…" The vicar's voice trailed off as the ghost no longer acknowledged his presence. The vicar wished he had thought through his theological arguments. How does one explain Christ to someone that perished before his resurrection?

He slowly made his way back to the cart in the dripping, frosty rain. Clutching his cross, it warmed his numb fingers, but he could not shake the crushing burden of inadequacy.

"May the Lord one day receive you in his bosom, Quintus Flavius," he whispered.

* * *

The Bodhisattva, 1987

The bodhisattva traversed the ocean. In his latest lifetime, now that he could shift his form at will, he found that it was the blue whale that best aligned best with his newfound vastness of perception. A human mind, like an eager hound, chased after ideas bound by cause and effect, tumbling one after the other in swift succession. Sharp and keen as it was, the mind is oblivious to the interconnected web of simultaneity, oblivious to the spacious peace permeating all. *Yoga is the cessation of the mind.* In another lifetime, the bodhisattva had studied the words of the wise Patanjali at the feet of the masters in the sweltering jungles, then pursued that cessation in the solitude of a cave in the snow-topped mountains. The blue whale's mind settled naturally into what a human struggled to achieve.

The deep waters felt like an embrace encompassing his massive body. He felt the call of abundance from a cloud of krill above. With a graceful sweep of his tail, he surfaced, opening his cavernous mouth to engulf them. The cool water rushed in, and he pressed it out through his baleen. Thus, a mass of beings were sent forward on their journey, just as he himself had journeyed on Earth for a long time by human reckoning. The ocean teemed with life—predators, and bounty alike. They moved along the complex web of currents as the calls of other whales reverberated for miles and miles. Now he traveled towards a faint but persistent beacon that lingered at the edge of his consciousness—and had in other lives, too.

At first, he experienced shapeless, uneasy flashes of imagery, like fragments of a dream. Then, as he lived, died, and was reborn, he achieved clarity and remembered the succession of lifetimes. The first thing that inspired his longing for freedom from the endless cycle of lives marked by selfishness and violence was the unexpected dissatisfaction he experienced as a highwayman, killing a Roman sentinel to impress a woman who had not been impressed. Then, there was his failed attempt—as a naïve young vicar—to reason with the sentinel's ghost. He had been inexplicably drawn to the sentinel by what he now understood as a karmic tie. The vicar had lived his life as a parish priest, serving Christ and growing in skill and wisdom. Since the vicar passed, the bodhisattva had studied yoga and prince Gautama's wisdom. He had been a Sufi mystic and a pilgrim—or a bum and a fool of God, depending on who was asked. He had served Christ in other guises. He always wore his compassion for those suffering in the vale of tears upon his breast. He had done his best to learn how best to offer succor to the helpless.

And now, at long last, he traversed the ocean to relieve the suffering of the one to whom he owed a karmic debt.

Close to the shores of Albion, the bodhisattva joyfully surfaced to blow, then slowed down and searched for the form of a man. He adjusted to the narrow, predatory keenness and all-consuming passion. He felt uncomfortable at first; however, the state of steady, undying awareness he lived in settled the unease, and thus he changed shape and became a man—an unremarkable man of forty or so years of age and healthy of body. He chose to wear plain, friendly features and a sandy mop of hair.

In his new form, the bodhisattva swam towards the sandy cove and emerged from the waves.

* * *

The bodhisattva strolled through the town cemetery, politely greeting the few passersby. A young couple pushing a stroller had left flowers at the neo-classical vault dominating the rows of headstones. The bodhisattva still recognized the Roman columns and the carved angels.

The Reardon family vault was well maintained. Judging from the names carved into the limestone, plenty of the industrialist's descendants still lived nearby. The inscription informed that Lieutenant John Michael Reardon lost his life in 1941 over the English Channel, defending freedom, at the age of twenty-one. The red poppies were likely meant to commemorate him.

The bodhisattva reached for a faint image of a young lieutenant with intense green eyes and a confident smile, wearing a tilted RAF side cap. "Fly free, wherever you are," he whispered. Douglas Reardon's name was displayed most prominently, as was fitting for the patriarch of the family.

Not even Reardon admonished the young vicar who failed to banish the Roman ghost, for nobody had been entirely sure how proper Christians were supposed to handle such things. When a 'papist' priest's discreet visit had proven equally fruitless, Reardon had cut his losses, and the port had been built farther south. The town prospered during the industrial age, then slowly declined. Now, however, the natural beauty of the area had started to attract a different kind of business. Visitors with an appreciation for nature and obscure history, those possessing a surplus of money and time for leisure, recently invigorated the town. Perhaps Tom the innkeep had unwittingly predicted the future. Far more people with "too much time and money on their hands" existed now than e in the 18th century.

The headstone of Harold and Ethel Thwaite stood nearby, sheltered by a row of yews. The handsome block of marble depicted an angel gracefully studying a book. A casual observer might wonder why a modest clerk and his wife had such a grand headstone. The friendship between Mistress Thwaite and Douglas Reardon had raised some eyebrows and had some tongues wagging, though she was much older and he was the one with money. Yet there's no accounting for taste, and stranger things have happened yet, the malicious and the cynical have often said. But the vicar had known that there was no truth to any innuendo.

Death had not diminished Ethel Thwaite's commitment to her husband of fifty years. As for Reardon, he enjoyed the friendly company of an intelligent woman with a hunger for stimulating conversation. A friend he could afford to show a more gentle and fanciful private side, in lieu of his driven and controlled public persona. Reardon kept his grief over Ethel's passing private, but he still ordered the handsomest headstone for Ethel and her husband, second only to his own planned family vault.

* * *

The bodhisattva walked the land. The coastal road still stretched through farmland and windswept cliffs in the dimming evening. The bay, he had learned from locals at the Shipwright's Arms, was a dangerous and confusing place of ghostly phenomena, jagged rocks, and odd currents. Reports of the ghost remained the same: it ignored all attempts to communicate, blew its bugle, and lit ghostly fires.

In the oblique light of the pale setting sun, a mass of fog began to rise from the sea. The cliff with its cracks was still the same as it had been when he had dashed towards the tower on the silent feet of a young highwayman. The ruined watchtower hadn't changed much since the vicar had observed it in the light of his lantern.

The ghost, however, had.

The bodhisattva squinted at the translucent figure, mingling with the misty strands of rising fog. The sentinel's eyes sank deeper into the tired, gaunt face. The lines around the mouth and on the forehead were more pronounced. The posture was rigid and strained.

This time, the bodhisattva wouldn't reveal his presence until he knew how to bypass the entrenched sentinel's suspicions. He retreated to the undying, expansive light of consciousness that was each and every soul's original home, no matter how obscured by the wild, violent storms of karma. Quintus Flavius, tireless in life, was beyond tired in death. The haunting questions of senselessness and lost opportunities had already started to whisper to him before the highwayman struck him down. Only duty to his empire anchored him. It had provided a purpose and made sense of the life he had lived. In the death he had still not completely registered, he clung to that purpose, taking pride in his steadfast commitment to his duty. The alternative, it seemed to the ghost, would be despair and madness, a descent into Tartarus to join others who had lost their honor.

The bodhisattva reached out to the fragmented memories of the serious, respectful adolescent at the sun-kissed vineyards and olive orchards of Tusculum, soon to be shipped to the chilly, alien Britannia with other recruits. A longing for vague dreams concerning a blue-eyed girl with a ribbon in her hair faded in time. Her face would not convince Quintus to leave his post. Those dreams had been replaced by a commitment to and camaraderie with other youths, whom Quintus always felt slightly separate from due to their rowdy, juvenile nature. Yet he was fond of them due to their shared hardships and the threat of death they faced together. Quintus tolerated cold, hunger, and lack of sleep without complaint, mastered his fear when facing death and developed pride in being the man who did as he said he would while serving under the banners of the legendary Legio XX Valeria Vitrix.

A face, less faded, stood out in the stream of memories: the centurion Tiberius Claudius Crispus, broad-shouldered with a puckered scar across his jaw and an unruly mop of thick, curly hair he struggled to shear neatly, swearing abundantly at the effort. The centurion welcomed the new recruits in Britannia and had made soldiers out of Quintus and his companions.

"Here in Britannia, warfare is different. The enemy won't meet you in an open field. They strike from shadows, lure you into unfamiliar terrain, and sever your line of communication and supplies. Do not underestimate them. They are of this land and they use it wisely."

The recruits marched, built fortifications, learned to meticulously maintain their equipment, and to use terrain to their advantage. Crispus understood that if men took pride in their toil, they would give their best. In this he showed his recruits what it meant to serve Rome, what it meant to be a legionary. When punishment was merited, Crispus didn't hesitate to mete it out, though never capriciously or unjustly. At the end of the day, he cared deeply about his soldiers and took responsibility for their well-being and survival.

The centurion was the kind of man Quintus had wanted to be. A man who could be relied upon, who knew exactly what he stood for. Quintus learned and never forgot, not even when his orders took his unit farther north, and he and Crispus parted ways.

When he reached the platform, the bodhisattva changed his form to best appeal to the sentinel. He flexed his broad shoulders and felt the scar stretch his skin at the jaw. He tucked his stubborn curls under the crested helmet and approached the ghost.

"*Salve, Quintus*," he said.

Quintus Flavius' eyes widened, and he snapped to attention. "*Centurio!*"

"At ease, *miles*, at ease," the bodhisattva answered in Crispus's gruff voice.

Quintus relaxed, and the bodhisattva put his hand on the ghost's shoulder. "Beautiful view."

"I suppose, *centurio*," Quintus answered. "I am accustomed to it. I have watched over it for so long."

The bodhisattva grunted in acknowledgment and motioned for Quintus to follow him to the edge of the platform. The soldiers watched the sunset in a comfortable silence.

He reached back to the times of the empire when the Romans marched all around the known world. The collective longings of the Romans in that era created a mind field called Elysium, which had slowly faded away, half-forgotten until, in later centuries, the fascination of artists and scholars breathed new life into it.

Elysium, Elysium!
A place of honor for the valorous!
A place of respite for the weary!
I'm calling to you, Elysium, on behalf of a son of Rome who much
deserves rest. I implore you to welcome him until he is ready to move on.

In the eternal light of his overlaying consciousness, there was the flicker of a lush field dotted with spring flowers and crystal springs. The battle standard of Quintus's legion was displayed over a prepared feast, but the young men gathered around had laid down their weapons for good. A temple adorned with Corinthian columns stood in the meadow. A blue-eyed girl smiled and poured them wine. A kindly old man served fruit from an overflowing horn of plenty. Who these souls had been in Quintus's times had long since scattered to the winds of karma on their own journeys. But these were the lingering fragments of a shared memory, once charged with emotion. Some of these souls had since grown wise and evolved beyond the mortal coil. They had answered the bodhisattva's ethereal call beyond matter and space, lending their support for his cause by granting his will a tangible form.

"You have been a good soldier, Quintus Flavius. You have done your duty impeccably, and carried your weariness without complaint. Gods know you are more of a Stoic than any one of those bleating philosophers. But now, it is time for your watch to end."

"*Centurio?*" A mixture of hope, relief, and fear animated Quintus' ghostly eyes.

"It can be frightening after so long. I was one of the lucky ones. I made it alive to retirement with nothing worse than this dent in my jaw to show for my warring years. By Jupiter, it scared me. All I knew was war. But things change. It's how the world grows, and so we change, too. It is part of a soldier's duty to lay down arms when his watch has ended."

The bodhisattva reached for Quintus' hands and clasped them in his own. "You did well, Quintus. You did very well."

"The empire?" Quintus asked. "What of Rome?"

"Long fallen," the bodhisattva grunted. Seeing Quintus's crestfallen face, he continued, "The empire will never be forgotten. It still rules minds and imaginations, if not lands. Its glory is eternal. But Rome no longer needs your vigil."

The Elysian Fields took shape in the sky. "Look there, Quintus. Look—there is your reward for your service."

Quintus smiled. "The Elysian Fields…"

"See, there is young Titus and Cassius. All your fallen comrades who served alongside you with honor."

Quintus's smile widened. "Marius has legs again!"

"And there's young Tullia pouring wine, see, and your old father with the cornucopia. Go to the banquet in your honor, go be with those you love. *Custodia tua perfecta est.* Your watch is over."

Quintus saluted the centurion one final time, then began to fade as he walked towards the people from his past who raised their hands in greeting. The bodhisattva watched as he laid down his weapons and armor, at the feast. A warm breeze carried the scent of cypresses until the Elysium faded away.

"Rest well, Quintus Flavius. Rest as long as you need. And then, when you are ready, journey on with my blessing," said the bodhisattva as the sun disappeared completely behind the horizon.

THE SINISTER SORCERER
MAKES A BELIEVER OUT OF SAM
by Ed Kratz

Sam Flat stood outside editor Nigel Hardcastle's door, holding the submissions he'd ordered by date received, with the oldest on top and the most recent at the bottom.

He'd resign today. His girlfriend, Alana, was Nigel's niece. She'd gotten Sam this position. Sam didn't believe that silly stuff, but the Magazine of the Mysterious had a huge circulation that would look great on Sam's resume.

If he wanted to be a serious journalist, he had to leave.

Nigel's door was open. Sam fidgeted from one foot to the other.

"Gird your loins and come in, my young, innocent assistant. "

Sam walked in. Various mystical creatures like tiny dragons, trolls, and unicorns filled the shelves on Hardcastle's walls. Who believed in this stuff?

Nigel smiled, removed the unlit pipe he kept in his mouth like a pacifier. "Please put the submissions down."

Sam struggled to find a spot to put the manuscripts down. As always, Nigel's desk looked like a tornado had just passed over it. Where could Sam put the sorted manuscripts?

"Why, right there."

Yes. A large space. Why hadn't he seen it before? Probably because the dumb walls caught his attention.

"So, you're thinking of leaving us?"

Sam jumped. Could the silly old man read his mind?

"Of course, I can't read your mind. If I did, I might take offense at being considered a 'silly old man'... You do not believe our magazine is legitimate?"

"Well, the website has a big red disclaimer on the home page that says 'for amusement purposes only.' "

"A legal requirement. What if someone found how to change their spouse into a frog on our site? Imagine an army of lawyers waiting to jump on that! Far too many to change into frogs."

"Yes," Sam said. "Sure." Then a submission he had placed at the bottom of the pile floated into Nigel's hands.

Sam searched for words. His eyes went from the pile to the manuscript, back and forth. "It floated. I mean. It floated. "

"Persistent, isn't he? Now you know why we only take paper submissions. Imagine a surly sorcerer submitting a cursed manuscript via the Internet."

"It floated…" Sam mumbled.

"Son, my dear Alana tells me you study journalism. Surely you can find more words."

Sam couldn't find any. Couldn't think of anything other than the floating submission.

Nigel turned to the manuscript. "'Salient Solutions from the Sinister Sorcerer.' Well, that sounds scary, doesn't it?"

Sam still couldn't move. Considering the levitating manuscript, it did sound scary. He was scared, and he wanted to quit. He should quit, but his journalist heart struggled with his fear. Was this nonsense real? His mind kept coming back to that floating.

"My dear lad, are you ill? You may go. I'll review these and we'll discuss them when you come back."

"It moved," Sam mumbled as he shuffled out. He thought again about quitting, but a small part of his mind pointed out that this could really be something to investigate.

* * *

Half an hour later, Sam tapped on Nigel's closed door. This was crazy. He had to quit. No answer. He tapped again. No answer.

"Hello," he called. A strange, loud, reverberating noise, sounding like a frog croaking, came from the room. "Do you need help?" Hearing another croak that somehow sounded desperate, Sam flung the door open and rushed in.

A huge frog sat on Nigel's desk.

"Help!" Sam screamed. "There's a frog in here!"

Sam backed away. He had to get out. He was done.

Just as he neared the door, the frog's croaking rose to a crescendo.

Sam crept to the desk.

The frog pointed with its tongue to the submission Nigel had been reading when Sam left.

The submission had 'Rejected' written in bright, bold letters across the top, along with the comment: 'Your advice, or solutions such as they are, are to turn evildoers into frogs. What is this, the Hebrew Holiday of Pesach, with the plague of the frogs?'

"I'll get help." Sam said. For a moment, he realized he was talking to the frog, but he didn't care. Before he could put the manuscript down, the writing changed to 'Accepted. You are a brilliant wizard.'

While Sam stared at the now accepted rejection, a mist covered the large frog. Gradually, the mist cleared, and Nigel showed up, crouched on his desk. He shook like a wet dog, and pieces of green splashed about.

'You want to be a journalist,' Sam repeated over and over in his mind. Frog. Man. Pieces.

He dodged some green.

"Don't worry about that. Frog is not catching. Give me a hand getting down."

Sam helped Nigel down, and the editor sat in his chair.

"Change me into a frog, will he? Perhaps he should be a rat. Not a frog. Right, Sam?"

Sam stared. Did he notice some frog clinging to Nigel?

"You are a quiet young lad. Never mind. I'll handle this petty performer with pretension. Still thinking of leaving our magazine?"

"You wouldn't... I mean—change me? Would you?"

"Into a frog? Why, I don't think my niece would like that. She would probably kiss you and change you back, anyway, wouldn't she? She's quite fond of you, I hear."

Alana was so beautiful. But Sam thought of that frog. "Alanna. Is she?"

"You're worried Alana might be studying magic. I would love Alanna to enter the family business. Alas, she finds the study of magic too challenging and prefers an easier field, like medicine." Nigel smiled. "You may go now, and rest assured, Alanna will not turn you into a frog if you displease her."

"Yes."

"You're still not thinking of leaving? I offer no threats."

"No, I'll stay," Sam said. As he walked out, he thought that this might just be the greatest break he could get in his journalistic career. But he still desperately hoped Alanna was fixed on pre-med. He hoped so, indeed.

THE PACK

by Raima Larter

The man, and the woman, too, had both become skeletons in their bed. The woman had been the one to feed Shep and to gather eggs from the chicken coop, but when it became clear that his bowl would no longer be filled, Shep started chasing and eating the chickens, at least the ones he could catch.

Shep was soon joined by other dogs, all of them left to fend for themselves since their people were also dead. They ran as a pack now, patrolling the valley and watching for the enemy. Long, pointed metallic monsters would, from time to time, zing across the sky before slamming into the hillsides and splitting open, spilling something that smelled of death.

The dogs began to discuss things. One dachshund pointed out that it was mostly insects, rodents, and other small furry things that had survived the attack. They lived in the left-behind places: mice in the barn, which had once held milk cows and saddle horses; rats in the chicken coop, which was raided by the fox soon after the metal monsters arrived; and spiders in the cellar, which the woman visited often, its jars of preserved, inaccessible food now covered with a thick layer of dust.

Dogs, cats, even foxes and birds survived, but large animals like the cows and horses had gone the way of the people. All that remained of the livestock were piles of bones in the corners of the barn.

Why some werespared and not others wasn't clear. Shep had a theory, which he explained to the other dogs: "The metal monsters are from outer space," he said, pointing at the night sky with his nose. "They come from there, beyond the moon."

Doxie, the dachshund, didn't agree. "That's ridiculous. Where do you get these ideas?"

"There are dogs out there, beyond the moon, see," said Shep. "They've come to find their own kind."

Doxie scoffed. "Space monsters? Really?"

Rixie, a curly labradoodle, shook her head. "You're wrong, Shep. I heard the monsters weren't from space at all. They came from the other side of the Earth."

"Where did you hear that?" Shep was incredulous and didn't really understand what the "other side" of the Earth might mean anyway. Clearly, the Earth had only one side—you could see the edge out beyond the tree line. Shep shook his head. Rixie had always been a bit naïve, and ever since her people died, she'd gotten much worse.

And so, the argument continued, day after day—when there was even time to talk, which wasn't much at all, since the dogs kept busy hunting small game. One of the cats tore open feed sacks in the barn, providing an unexpected bounty, at least for a while.

Although Shep continued to insist his theory about space invaders was the truth, it didn't matter. Their people were dead, killed by the sleek pointy objects with fire for a tail, which really did seem to come out of nowhere. The dogs were on their own.

Shep, who had always been good at herding other animals, now used those skills to rally the other dogs to a singular cause. He urged the pack to keep hunting. "We need to do whatever we can to stay alive," he said, although sometimes he wondered if it might have been better to go wherever his people had gone.

* * *

Shortly after the first attack, when the man was still alive, he called to Shep from his bed. Shep was already worried since the woman had stopped moving, grown cold and stiff, and now the man had been in bed for days.

"Come here, boy," the man called. Shep walked closer, his tail hanging but wagging slowly. "Listen to me, Shep: go out to the pasture and get the cows." The man coughed several times. "It's time for the cows to come back to the barn. To come home."

Shep sat at the side of the man's bed, his tail swishing across the floor as he listened, amazed that he understood everything the man was saying. In the past, he'd known a few words: walk, sit, eat, and cows. That last one was his signal to get to work—time to herd the cows and make them go wherever the man directed.

Shep was good at his job; he'd done it for years. But that day, as the man lay on his stack of pillows, pointing out the window to the sheep in the field, Shep heard even more words: "pasture," and then "barn," and then "home," and suddenly the full meaning of what the man was saying, had always said, fell into place. Shep heard a complete thought, not just isolated words.

He barked and moved his head toward the man's hand, knowing he would scratch behind his ears and rub his head, like he always did. And, of course, that's exactly what the man did. "You're a good boy, Shep. You know that?"

Shep lifted his head and looked into the man's glazed eyes. "Yes," he said.

The man's eyes grew round, and he drew back. "Wha—?"

"Yes," Shep repeated. "Shep, good boy."

"Oh my!" The man propped himself up on an elbow, which triggered a coughing fit. Shep ran across the room, grabbed a tissue from the box on the dresser with his teeth, and brought it to the man. He coughed again, pressing the tissue against his mouth, and when he pulled it away, Shep saw a dark spot and smelled something familiar.

"Blood?" Shep asked.

The man's eyes grew even wider, and he lay back on the pillow, staring for a long moment. "I—I must be hallucinating. Dogs don't talk."

But Shep knew the man was wrong. He didn't know what "hallucinating" meant, but he knew dogs could talk. They'd always talked, with nips and barks and head butts. And now they could talk in a better way. Well, one dog could, anyway.

As it turned out, though, it wasn't just Shep who had developed this ability. A few weeks after the man stopped moving in his bed and his body grew cold and stiff, Doxie came loping into Shep's yard.

Doxie stopped at the front porch and shouted, "Shep!" Normally, Doxie would bark when he came over to play. He'd never called Shep by name, but here he was, grinning and wagging his tail. "Shep!" he repeated.

"Doxie," Shep said. "You talk?"

Doxie leapt up and turned in a circle, his tongue lolling out. "Doxie talk! Doxie talk!" He turned and pointed his nose toward the gate. "Rixie talk too."

And then there was Rixie, zipping through the open gate, panting. "Rixie run," she said. "A long way."

Rixie lived on the other side of the field, the one where the cows always grazed. Shep agreed—it really was a long way. Rixie was a good runner, though, but what was immediately clear to Shep was this: Rixie could talk, too, just like he and Doxie could.

In those early days, when the man and woman were not yet fully skeletons in the bed, the dogs practiced talking, teaching each other words they'd learned from their people. One of Shep's favorite words that he knew, but Doxie and Rixie didn't, was 'moon'. He'd learned it from the woman, who sang a lovely song about it. One night, as the golden disk rose into the sky above the far hill, he called Doxie and Rixie over, pointing with his nose. "That is the moon," he said. "Moon—I love that word."

Shep's sentences improved, and he noticed that, over time, Doxie's sentences did too, as did Rixie's. They were learning. He didn't know why, but Shep and his pack did not really have time to dwell on what was happening to them. Even though he no longer had cows to herd back to the barn, there was still work to do. When Shep had first come upon the cows' bodies, all huddled together at the back of the barn, he'd worried that Doxie and Rixie would get sick, too, but it never happened.

* * *

One day, everything changed. A high-pitched whistling sound caught the attention of the dogs, who all came running. It was another of the monsters, streaking through the sky, heading toward the soft ground near the apple orchard. It slid into the soil, gouging up dirt as it careened between the trees, toppling a few of them. This time, unlike the other metallic beasts that had plunged in, the pointy monster remained intact and did not split open. Instead, it lay there in a smoking heap a short distance from the barn, clicking as it cooled.

Doxie barked at the beast, pulling back and baring his teeth. Rixie lay on the ground, trying to cover her muzzle with her paws, whimpering.

Shep let out a big sigh. It was up to him to investigate. These two were not going to be any help at all. And the rest of the pack was useless as well—they'd all run off as soon as the metallic beast had crashed into the orchard. Shep slowly approached the shiny object and sniffed at it. It exuded heat from its gleaming surface, but it didn't smell like anything. He lifted a paw and tapped.

A panel flipped open on the side of the monster. Shep leapt back as it unfolded and ejected a flat object with a glass screen. Shep had seen a screen like that before. The man, and sometimes the woman too, once sat in their chairs late into the night, staring at strange markings on screens like this. A loud beep came from the flat object, and it began to flicker, and suddenly, there, on the screen, was the image of a man. Not the man Shep had known and loved—not any of the men the other dogs had been so attached to—but a man, nonetheless, and he was staring, blinking his eyes rapidly, and speaking in a strange language that sounded like barking to Shep.

Shep backed away. "Who are you?" he shouted. "Where did you come from?"

The man on the glass screen laughed and pointed toward Shep, then turned and waved his hands. Another man appeared in the glass, leaning down, staring at Shep. He, too, broke into a laugh. He smiled at the first man and spoke in a rapid-fire guttural language that sounded nothing like the language Shep's old masters spoke. These two were not at all like the man who once rubbed his head and the woman who fed him. These two were not Shep's people.

These two were clearly the enemy.

* * *

Byers couldn't believe what he was seeing: dogs! They should not have survived the drone attacks, but there they were, prancing around in front of the camera he and Matthews sent in on an observation probe.

"Hey!" he shouted to Matthews, who was bent over the lab bench, testing air samples the drones had gathered from the blast site. "Come take a look," he said, waving Matthews over to the monitor.

His colleague leaned down and broke into a big grin. "How in the world did they survive?" Byers shrugged and shook his head as Matthews reached toward the keyboard. "Are we getting any sound?"

Matthews unmuted the mic on the observation probe and turned up the volume. At first, it sounded like ordinary barking and yipping—like ordinary dog sounds. But then—

"What the hell?" Byers stood up so fast his rolling chair shot backward across the room, colliding with the lab bench. He stared at Matthews. "Those dogs are talking."

Matthews nodded and pressed his lips together. "Yep. I'd say that was strange enough, but just listen to the language they're using."

Byers started to shake, unsure of what was happening. Not only were these dogs speaking—they were speaking Russian.

* * *

One of the foxes had taken to walking on its hind legs. Shep spotted it as it left the chicken coop, walking on two legs and clutching three eggs to its furry chest. It disappeared into the woods, but returned soon after, loping along on all fours the way a normal fox should.

Shep hid behind the gooseberry bush next to the coop to get a better view. The fox entered the hen house, immediately stood up on its two hind legs, and walked toward the back. It reached up to where Shep knew the chickens built a nest on the back wall, a place that neither Shep nor the fox could usually reach.

The sight brought a sudden stab of sadness to Shep's chest. He remembered how the woman had gathered eggs each morning, from this very spot, just before she brought Shep's food to his bowl.

The fox walked out of the coop, clutching three more eggs close, and hobbled off through the woods on two legs. Shep came out from behind the gooseberry bush and dashed into the coop. The chickens had not even been touched—they were still clucking, very much alive. Content even. The sound of their clucking and scratching at the ground brought a cascade of memories: the woman and her egg-gathering, of course, but also the man, who sat by the fire at night. Shep loved curling up on the rug before the hearth while the man sat in a chair, rustling large sheets of paper, turning them one by one.

The woman sat near the fire as well, moving long spikes of metal in elaborate patterns through piles of colorful yarn. She created the most amazing things: blankets, pillow covers, sweaters for the man, even a little round mat she placed under Shep's food bowl.

Shep thought of the fox again and wondered if maybe he, too, could stand up on his hind legs. Maybe if he practiced walking like the fox, he could also begin to do the things the woman and man did to keep the farm running.

After all, when their people died, the pack needed to find a way to survive, so they had learned to do so. They'd learned to talk. And they could learn other things. Shep was sure of it.

Tending the farm was never something Shep wanted, but he understood now: his job before had been herding cows and sheep, but now all the farm work fell to him. Well, he and the other dogs. And maybe the cats. But, really, would cats ever do anything for others? Probably not.

Time to give it a try: he placed his front paws on the wall of the chicken coop and struggled to get up on his hind legs.

He was upright, but it felt awful, and his back hurt. A lot! And to make matters worse, as soon as he removed his paws from the wall, he lost his balance and toppled over. He tried again, removing just one of his front paws from the wall this time. It worked a little better, but not for long. Soon, he was back on all fours again.

Maybe the fox was a lot smarter than Shep. He didn't want to believe that, or admit it, but maybe Shep, who was just a sheepdog, could never do what a fox—or a man—could do.

He wandered away from the coop toward the garbage pile, and there was Rixie, digging through a heap of rotting vegetation, probably looking for rats or something to eat. Shep looked away, shame washing through him. This is what he and the other dogs had been reduced to. If only he and Rixie were smart enough to do what the fox had done— walk upright and gather eggs—maybe dogs would no longer need to dig through garbage.

"Rixie!" Shep said, running up. "You should've seen what I just saw! There's a fox who's figured out something we might be able to use."

Rixie looked up, her muzzle covered with dirt. "What do you mean? Use for what?"

He sniffed at the rotting garbage. Rixie didn't seem to mind, but the whole thing made Shep angry as well as sad. "Come on—come with me and watch what the fox does at the chicken coop. You're not going to believe this."

* * *

Byers convinced Matthews to call Dr. Marjorie Owens, the scientist at NIH whose team developed the neurotoxin. She agreed to come to their lab. Army Special Forces loaded her team's toxin into guided missiles intended for the Russian military base just beyond the border with Finland, but something had clearly gone very wrong.

"We think that storm that came up suddenly blew the drones off course," Byers explained to Dr. Owens. "Take a look at the images our observation drones are recording."

She bent down to look at Byers' screen. In the countryside near Vyborg, dogs were not only talking, but now walking on their hind legs.

"What are they doing?" she asked, frowning. "It looks like they're cooperating on some sort of task? Extraordinary."

"Exactly," Byers said. "We need to contact McAfferty—now."

She crossed her arms. "Do we really need to involve the top brass? I'm getting very uncomfortable with this," she said, color draining from her face.

Byers glanced at Matthews. They'd talked about this, argued really. The message from the Pentagon was clear: to stop a ruthless enemy, sometimes you need to be just as ruthless. He didn't like it, but this was war.

* * *

Shep had always been good at herding the man's sheep and cows, and he now turned his attention to the dogs. "Come on, everyone!" Shep shouted as he urged the group toward the barn's outer wall. "Get those paws up there and try to stand upright. You can do it—just keep working at it!"

The dogs had been practicing for at least an hour when Doxie stopped, pointing his nose and front paw at the barn door. "Look at that!"

Shep watched two cats exit the barn. They dragged two empty feed sacks they'd torn open weeks ago out of the barn and into the chicken coop. Minutes later, they were back again, hauling the bags out. The sacks were now bulging with something. Eggs? Could be.

Rixie laughed. "Why didn't we think of that?" she said. "Those cats are really crafty—you don't need to walk on your hind legs to gather a lot of eggs. You just need to use a bag."

Doxie tipped his head to the side. "But wait. What if all the eggs get taken? And what if the chickens die? Isn't that where chickens come from—eggs?"

Shep nodded. "I see your point, Dox. Maybe we should get one of the feed sacks, collect eggs, and keep them away from the foxes and cats. If we want more chickens, we need to intervene."

Rixie ran into the barn and came out with an empty feed sack. "Let's get started!"

* * *

Vyborg, Russia (AP) – *This week marks two years since a freak hurricane in the North Atlantic devastated the region near the border between Finland and Russia. Access to the countryside near the village of Vyborg, about an hour's train ride from St. Petersburg, remains restricted due to a possible nuclear accident in the area. U.S. government officials believe the plant suffered a catastrophic failure during the storm, but the Kremlin denies that any nuclear accidents have occurred anywhere in Russia. Every investigator who has gone into the area has returned very ill, experiencing internal bleeding, massive organ failure, and eventual death, so Russian authorities have sealed off the region.*

Officials at the Pentagon refused to comment, referring press inquiries to the Russian embassy. When questioned about any connection between the sealed-off region and Russia's continued aggression against Ukraine and the West, the Russian ambassador did not respond.

* * *

The rats began to build something. At first, Shep thought it was some sort of structure to live in, but when they used the contraption to launch stones at the cats, he realized what they had developed: a weapon. It was a confusing mess of strings and ropes and sticks. The rats loaded small stones into it, launching them at the cats whenever they tried to invade the rats' territory.

Shep hid behind the gooseberry bush, watching all this unfold. The rats squeaked at each other and waved their paws around as they rolled the stones toward the catapult, pulled it back, and let the stone fly toward an invading cat. He listened carefully to the squeaking and realized the rats were talking, too, although Shep couldn't understand them.

The rats were smart, but Shep knew he and his pack were smarter. As he watched the little furry creatures launch another attack on their enemies, the cats, it gave him an idea: maybe he and his pack could create a weapon too. Maybe he and the pack could launch an attack on their enemy, pelting the pointy metal monsters with stones until they were destroyed. It was the least the pack could do. The enemy may have killed Shep's people, and Doxie's and Rixie's too, but they weren't going to get away with it. Shep and his pack were going to stand up for their land.

* * *

The Pentagon brass was called in, and here they were, visiting Byers' and Matthews' lab with a whole contingent of troops. Dr. Owens was still there and stood to the side, her lips clamped tightly shut, tapping one foot nervously.

General McAfferty gestured at Matthews' computer and turned to Dr. Owens. "How could this happen? Didn't you folks test the bio-weapon on animals?"

She sagged forward slightly. "Yes, General, we did test it on animals. Rats, mainly, but also mice and birds. As you know, the Army wanted a toxin that would affect only humans."

Dr. Owens clenched her hands into fists. Byers looked at Matthews, raising his eyebrows. Clearly, something had gone wrong with the toxin itself, but ordering the guided missile attack just as a storm kicked up was perhaps a worse mistake. The toxin was meant for the Russian army depot located east of Vyborg, but the brass did not seem the least bit concerned about the Russian civilians they'd mistakenly killed.

The General shook his head and sighed. "Well, if you tested it on animals, Dr. Owens, you must have noticed some ill effects."

She shook her head. "No, General, we did not. If anything, the drug we'd developed seemed to improve their health." She gave him a weak smile. "In fact, the rats who received the largest dosage were able to master the maze puzzle we use as a standard measure in half the usual time. It was amazing!"

Matthews frowned. "Wait—could it affect dogs the same way? I mean—could it enhance their intelligence somehow?"

She shrugged. "It's possible. We just didn't think to test for that."

The General turned on his heel and strode toward the door. As he waited for his aide to open it for him, he turned back. "Well, Doctor, it looks like you have a real-life test opportunity right here. Perhaps we should send in some investigators to check out these dogs." He stepped through the door, but turned around and came back in. "Matthews— I'm assigning you to set this up. You'll receive detailed orders soon, but one more thing: check the other animals in the area as well. There's no telling how wide this thing has spread."

* * *

Washington (AP) *Investigators from the Union of Concerned Scientists held a press conference today, summarizing their suspicions that something other than a nuclear accident has occurred in the region near Vyborg, Russia, which has been inaccessible for months. The Kremlin continues to deny that any nuclear accident occurred, providing data that show no radioactivity in the region. The IAEA, the international nuclear monitoring agency, agrees, stating that no signs of a nuclear accident have been observed.*

Requests for comment by Pentagon authorities, including General McAfferty of the Joint Chiefs of Staff, were yet again referred to the Russian embassy. "We all know the Russians are experts at disinformation,"

McAfferty said. *"This situation is no different. The Russians are hiding something, that much is clear."*

When informed of General McAfferty's claims, the Russian Ambassador responded, "It is ironic that the U.S. accuses Russia of disinformation, when we all know the United States is a master at such things."

* * *

Shep gathered the pack and assigned jobs: Rixie and a black Lab named Boris, who had wandered in looking for food, hauled logs from an old broken-down fence to an area near the pointy metal monster. The screen, which stuck out from the side, still buzzed from time to time and showed images of people, but if Shep's plan worked, they would soon smash the thing. Doxie and some of the cats, who had been convinced to help, dragged rope from the barn and rolled heavy stones toward the contraption. The rats, curious little fellows, came to watch and were soon helping out as well, waving their paws around to show the dogs and cats how to put the weapon together.

Just as they were about to launch the first stone at the enemy lodged beneath the apple trees, a half dozen human-looking figures came over the hill. They were dressed in white and had metal and glass contraptions on their heads, tubes snaking around to packs on their backs.

Doxie shouted, "It's the enemy!" and started to run away.

"Stop!" Shep grabbed Doxie by the scruff of the neck with his teeth, dragging Doxie back to the frontline. "We must defend our land. We can't run." He knew, now, that he had been right all along. These creatures vaguely resembled the people who had once cared for him and the other dogs, but they were not the same at all. He wasn't sure who those men he'd seen on the screen were, but these creatures were clearly the enemy. And what's more, it was obvious his original theory was right: these white-clad beings in helmets were aliens from somewhere beyond the moon.

* * *

Byers and Matthews were hunched over the monitor in the lab. After a brief firefight with Russian forces, U.S. Army forces in haz-mat suits had entered the region near Vyborg. Video and audio from their helmet cams streamed into the lab. Dr. Owens pulled up a third chair and was sitting to the side, watching and tapping her toe again.

She crossed her arms and turned away. "It appears those suits are protecting our soldiers from the toxin, but what about civilians in the area? Didn't you folks consider them?"

Matthews clenched his teeth, seething. People like her, bleeding hearts everywhere, just didn't understand what they were up against. If the Russians were allowed to continue their attacks, world peace was at stake. It was just like with Hiroshima—sometimes the unthinkable had to be thought, and you had to do the thing you said you never would, to stop something worse from happening.

Byers stood up fast. "What the—?"

He pointed at the screen. There, near the observation drone, was a row of dogs, all standing on their hind legs behind some sort of contraption made of logs and rope. A blood-curdling roar came from the group of creatures as one large dog yanked on the rope, launching a boulder toward the approaching soldiers.

Cats began to swarm around the dogs. As the boulder slammed into one soldier, they leapt onto the others, clawing at their uniforms, yowling and screaming in Russian.

"What are they saying?" Dr. Owens asked.

Byers flipped through his Russian-English dictionary and looked up, his eyes wide. "They are saying, 'We will defend our country. You will die.'"

Dr. Owens frowned. "How did you translate that so fast?"

He shrugged. "I've been listening in on the cats and dogs for a while." He held up a notebook, covered with scribbled words. "It probably would have been easier if I'd actually paid attention during my Russian course in training."

"Oh no!" Dr. Owens rushed toward the screen, tapping at it. "Look!"

And there, flickering on the screen, was an image they'd all feared, but never expected: two soldiers on the ground, their uniforms ripped open.

She turned on the two men. "How does it feel now? Our own soldiers are being exposed to the toxin. Did anybody think about them?"

Matthews glared. "I could ask you the same thing. When you took the contract, didn't you think about how your research would be used?" He pointed at the screen. "Didn't you worry that your work might come back to haunt you someday?"

* * *

Vyborg, Russia (AP) Reports have begun to pour in from regions near this small Russian town located close to the border with Finland. Speculation about a possible nuclear accident here in recent months has expanded to include reports of strange effects on animals and wildlife in the region.

"We saw a fox walking on its hind legs the other day," said Tatiana Novorsky, a resident whose farm lies just outside the sealed-off region. "My husband tried to capture it, but it ran off with a burlap bag stuffed with something bulky. Only later did we find that the fox had stolen two of our chickens."

In addition to Ms. Novorsky's claims, other reports have been received involving rats, mice, and even cats behaving strangely. Neither U.S. authorities nor the Kremlin provided any further information about this, both stating that such stories were obvious hoaxes.

XX 1401   BAD DOG

His Name was Envy
By Tony Daly

The dog lay uncomfortably on the ground,
green fur sodden, matted, tangled, with
young fleas building adobes overlooking
patchwork plains of raw-exposed skin.

His green muzzle in constant irritation
sniffing, sneezing, growling, snorting,
aggravated by a parasitic hermit
squatting in his spacious nasal passages.

His green ears under development
with a quaint city center and an explosion
of townhouses planned for well-to-do mites
raising families along his picturesque canals.

His eyes clouded a hazy greenish-grey,
blind to the larger world around him.
His mind only ventured within,
focused on self-suffering, hunger, pain;
his wants to be somebody—anybody else.

The dog lay uncomfortably on the ground
being pet by a gentle breeze he couldn't feel,
protected by a majestic tree he couldn't see,
surrounded by a field of wildflowers he couldn't smell,
with birds singing a rapturous tune he couldn't hear.

The dog lay uncomfortably on the ground
waiting for his master's glorious return,
but it had been over two thousand years,
so he dreamed of what he had lost,
thought of the pain he had suffered,
wished for a life beyond his mortal flesh,
and waited for his name to be called once again.

LITTER LIFE
By Stefano Ronchi

25.09.24: Well, dear diary whom I have never before used, I simply must chronicle this frankly unbelievable turn of events: here I was, wallowing in my writer's block, unable to come up with anything except rhymes for inappropriate (says you!) anatomical parts and/ or their bi-products, when the newsreel provides what I so fragrantly lacked: a cat! A mind-numbingly gigantic cat has been sighted!

Now, it is nowhere near April, and as far as I know, I am not dreaming nor on any hallucinogenic substances, so unless someone is playing a game of Hack all World News, what is now immortalised in my downloads must have been birthed from a lucid mind, right? Let's see if the morrow's sun shines true on these matters, or be it just a figment of the moon's gibbous smile.

26.09.24: Mr Tomorrow brought a steaming plate of Continued Insanity, seasoned liberally with Outrageousness! It is true: everything, everyone and anyone is reporting this. Joe Blog swears on his mother's grave (may she live long and true) it is real. Mad McHermit, living under a rock, can tell you it's as true as his talking cave rat friends—*It. Is. A. Fact!*

Calling it a gigantic cat, though, is unfair: more like a Cosmic Cat, CC for short (sadly, a coining birthed by more enterprising beings than I). Calling it gigantic is also an understatement: Godzilla, Titans, Cyclopean horrors from humanity's feverish dreams? Eat your hearts out, for this CC makes you look like my cousin's toys! A mountain in feline form, whiskers a concatenation of freight trains, eyes the size (or larger?) of stadiums…words fail to describe its sheer size.

So, let me focus on something that is fair: cosmic fits it to a tee. Its body glimmers with a faint translucence, while mesmerising patterns of alien energy swim in the ocean of its fur, starlight swirling in the lakes of its eyes… very impressive.

What is unclear is what it wants: it has been pacing the Sahara desert, but why? In search of what? For now, it is anyone's wild speculation.

27.09.24: As if things could not get any pottier, the CC was looking for a place to go potty! You and I read that right: it came, it saw, then it did its business and flew away into deep, dark space. Being an obviously backwater planet, our technology failed to track it, as it seemed to simply dissipate shortly after leaving our blue litter tray—blissfully, its nether regions were perpetually shrouded in an obscuring nebula throughout its whole visit, for I don't think I was prepared for graphic footage of its cloaka unloading, nevermind the other bit's uncurling! Thankfully, the number two looks more like a rather large heap of raw metal than what you'd expect an animal (is it even an animal?) should produce. The number one, a sort of milky, ominously bubbling body of water.

So, is that it? A random toilet break on an unfathomable journey? All manner of scientists are already buzzing about the remains, Earth's smartest flies feasting on the residue of a galactic god.

11.10.24: After two weeks, with the world holding its breath in bated anticipation, what do our wisest minds tell us?

"The creature's remains are extremely toxic and radioactive. Further investigation is required to understand what exactly they are."

Which is utterly hilarious: oh, vaulted humans we be, unable to even comprehend a stellar visitor's offloads! For now, at the very least, the buzzing continues unabated, so who knows where it will lead.

11.11.24: The CC is back! After keeping us waiting and wondering if it would ever grace us again, wonder no more, we shall! Or rather, the CCs, for it has brought two new friends to play!

11.11.24: Well…that's not so good. The first CC (just pure guesswork, as they all look identical) has returned to the Sahara Desert. Yet, the others have selected more problematic areas: one gauges up the lush Amazonian rainforest, the other rips up the fertile plains of China. Beyond the untold damage they cause by simply prancing about, if they use said areas as litter trays…I'm no expert, but didn't the experts say their gifts were highly toxic and radioactive?

20.11.24: It's confirmed: vast swathes of our blue planet's green pigmentation are now a decidedly ashy grey, despite every singular government's efforts to minimise the damage and remove the offending produce —even then, remove to where? Transporting such dangerous substances to more remote areas is, in itself, causing deaths and more ecological damage.

People are starting to feel nervous, wonder shifts to fear: if this pattern keeps repeating, if more CCs turn up... how long before our beautiful Earth is an inhospitable, barren lump?

14.3.25: Three more visits: always only three CCs (colossal mercies and all that), but that is more than enough. The ecological damage is... catastrophic. I mean, we're not yet at apocalypse levels, especially with the CCs always targeting the same area so long as their business is removed in a timely manner, but predictions are not rosy: maybe another ten years of this, and you can kiss goodbye to a lush(ish), vibrant planet. Who'd have thought that it wouldn't be us humans to usher Earth into that desolate future?

And that is why an army from all the worldly powers was amassed, waiting to shoo off the China CC when next it visits, make it clear that this is our planet, our turf, and they can go find another litter tray, thank you very much!

15.03.25: To say that things went poorly would be an understatement: the army was decimated without any gain. We were spared direct footage from the news. Still, worldwide communication being what it is, plenty came through on the web: planes death-locking onto the CC with a carpet of explosions to only enrage it into swiping them into terminal fireworks; rivers of tanks barraging it with untold shells, then suddenly targeting emptiness, the CC having pounced high, before crashing back down in an earthquake that was felt throughout Asia. Humanity's might was just one big cat toy.

Worse, all the CCs congregated together to see what the ruckus was about, and had a little play-fight before departing, which, admittedly, looked quite adorable, but wouldn't you know it? When titanic, world-defying creatures roll and pounce about, they create lots of havoc, death, and destruction.

12.04.25: The CCs are due back any day, and a drastic decision has been made: desperate times call for desperate measures, so it looks like humanity will bring out its final trump card: the A-bomb. Three atomic bombs, to be precise, targeted only at the Sahara CC, all to be sent from good ol' USA. Of course, vanity dictates we must lead on this, a decision aided and abetted by plenty of fence-sitters and "I would but I've got silo cramps" around the table of Ultimate World Power.

Is it the right move? Are we just poking the hornets' nest?

Why am I asking that? I am but a humble chronicler! The world has gone tits-up, and I'm here for the ride, baby. Fear, ecstasy, sorrow, doubt… let us mix them all up in one big cauldron, and ride those missiles Doctor Strangelove style!

15.04.25: This is it. The CCs are back. We shall soon know if the atom bomb is mightier than the cosmic cat.

15.04.25: Only in America is there a silo a kilometre from here, which sent a steaming hot missile straight at the CC! Even from here, the triumvirate of death could be seen, a misshapen false Sun struggling to rise from its mother's torn womb. But its CC sibling was the stronger, tearing apart the nascent apparition, and now it is really, really pissed.

Somehow, through some cosmic juju magic, feline tracking, or similar bull, the CCs know where those missiles came from, and all three are rampaging across each of the insolent attacking areas. It won't be long. I've lived as I've lived, I regret many things, yet I

Not hide they're here I'll see myself

An account of First Contact, Year 2025 AD, year 0 PC

* * *

02.03.2030, attempt 432: Isolation of the Cosmic Foci's alien particles continues to prove too transient to yield real benefits. Introduction of catatonic agitators has increased safety margins by 42%, yet the CF's binding particles, *ryle, arka,* and *sorma* continue to collapse within 0.0023s of separation, making reassembly impossible. The CF's energy particle *zion* remains both a problem and a possible solution, retaining its atavistic quantum charge indefinitely. Yet, its discharge requires the homoeostatic safety membranes to decontaminate for 24 hours, thus stopping any further experiments in the interim.

However, there is *no time*: worldwide society is at an optimistic 97% collapse gradient; war and conflict have engulfed 75% of humanity; food and potable water resources are insufficient to sustain even the scraps of what remains; and global research on any means of survival was halted as of 27.02.2030. The Feline Cosmic Phenomena will reappear within a predicted range of 25 to 28 days.

We must succeed.

05.03.2030, attempt 435: Renewed focus on energy particle *zion* and extrapolation into its baser elements *ka*, *lo*, and *ri*: previous attempt by cousin site Orion caused it and the surrounding 5 kilometres to sustain a Photon Disassembling Event, all data and backups lost. Our Patron has managed to *recover* 85.3% of the experiment's methodology, and the error now seems so obvious! Crude, positronic separation caused cascading photon reverberation until PTE was achieved. By instead tricking the elements via quantum superimposition, it should be possible to reassemble energy particle *zion* into a self-contained state!

06.03.2030, addendum: *Why* won't they *listen*? Paralysis of their amygdala leads my illustrious colleagues to wish for safer alternatives. *There. Is. No time!* This must occur *now*.

Yet, spineless as they may be, they're no fools: I'm being watched and occluded from acting.

10.03.2030, attempt 436: *Success!* At a cost: Henry Pengleton, my brightest assistant, is no more. Through ducts to the inner vibrationary shield, hacking directly into the membrane's synapses and opening a Transitory Bladder Retainer to transfer a few drops of CF into the necessarily programmed quantum box, before initiating the main experiment sequence by hand, it worked: he was dead as soon as the TBR opened, so we prepared a very lethal and painless toxin to take once his job was done.

What a *magnificent* cacophony of alarms went off to signal his triumph! Everyone scrambled to see what was happening, and while my *whimpering* colleagues stood ashen-faced, I took control. Energy particle *Zion* is now in a stable, directable form, increasing our ability to conduct experiments by an order of magnitude.

15.03.2030, attempt 500: *Failure* and more *failure.* Quantum superimposition was initiated on the binding particles *ryle, arka,* and *sorma,* yet it seems their bond somehow transcends the laws of relativity, and cannot be so easily replicated. Various structures, superstructures, and nanostructures were hypothesized and applied, yet they all failed to prevent their collapse. *All* manner of organic, inorganic, and imaginary agents have been utilised in an attempt to subvert or substitute for the unknown factors that retain the binding particle's cohesion, to *no avail.*

17.03.2030, addendum: Our Patron passed us an ultimatum: it transpires that all research had been halted due to every resource diverted towards the Perpetual Stasis Program, where survival of humanity is set aside in favour of a few elites waiting out the FCP's visits, logic dictating that once Earth is completely covered in their CF, they will lose interest and leave, so that said elites may emergence from their cryogenic sleep using specially designed protective suits, and leave for new horizons.

I thought that writing it would deny the utter *lunacy* of it. Still, it remains utter *trash*: Earth will be at such levels of toxicity that its so-called "Invincishells" will be unable to filter any usable air, let alone resist the incalculable radioactive and esoteric energies ravaging the surface! Earth itself will likely *collapse* under the energetic and gravitational forces at play before it can even reach such intolerable levels!

Our Patron warns us that we may have even less time than calculated, as what remains of the Global United States is dismantling the network of untraceable accounts, spy satellites, and undercover operatives keeping us safe from detection.

20.03.2030, attempt 1033: We've been working at a non-stop, *frenetic* rate, using all manner of stimulants to keep going, to reach a unique, singular conclusion: *everything* has been utilised. There is no substance, device, or solution available to our current level of technological or mental advancement that can successfully enable us to recombine the CF into clean, harmless elements. It is *over.*

22.03.2030, addendum: After prehaps too manie (or not enogh? Or just nough?) narcotic or/nd intoxictin substancles while we crasheddd throug a miasmai of despare and despondendency and generally feeeeeling sorrai for rselves and inking who lives a crap might ass wellk enjoy ourshelfes *and*d crossuing a *lot* (enough itilicisied iss too muvch at the momjent, oooh soiler!) of tavboos, abnd just gettring reasdy for the wend of timesa qend of all humanuity this is it aend of the kline, even now perthaps feedling a tiny bit the trepercusdsions of it all enoughf typing stop srtop S*ytop not the itili stuop afuligaertiybv*

23.03.2030, addendum: The anti...everything drugs have taken effect. A bit. As I was saying, I saw everything around me that soon would not be, my reflection in some broken mirror, my hands, trembling before me...and I sawed one off.

Quite painlessly (I wonder for how long, once these very strong painkillers wear off), using one of the laser saws we use for the lab work: switch it on, wave your hand through it, hand was on, snip snap, hand is off.

Made me vaguely recall a film...but, the point is: I'm going to use my hand for the next attempt. We've tried everything except us, us humans. Just need to recoup enough of my colleague's faculties, as I quite literally need more hands on this, and it shall be done.

24.03.2030, attempt 1034: *It worked!* Binding particles *ryle, arka,* and *sorma* remained detached yet utilised my human tissue to retain integrity long enough for energy particle *zion* to be applied to begin matter reassembling and obtain pure, harmless water vapour!

24.03.2030, addendum: After everyone's ecstasy, the stark reality hit us: we will need a larger test subject to see what the maximum human-to-vapour conversion is when applied to a larger CF sample. Lots are being arranged to decide who the sample will be.

24.03.2030, addendum: Wilfred was the brave sacrifice that fate picked. Let it not be in vain.

24.03.2030, attempt 1035: *It. Was. In. Vain!* The conversion ratio is approximately 1 human per 1 kilogram of CF. It would be impossible to reverse the damage of even one FCP visit, let alone the accumulation of all visits so far, and time is too short to streamline the process into a more efficient exchange. Must we be Icarus, to fall after getting so close?

26.03.2030, addendum: I refuse to believe that what we've done is pointless. While most of them fall into more despondent decadence, three colleagues and I are what remain of Humanity's Hope. There is something here, a solution. We feel it nagging at our prefrontal cortex, nibbling on those brain stems in the hopes of causing a spark...

27.03.2030, addendum: They're right. We are right. We've been trying to convert CF, but it is *us* that need to be converted. We must become able to metabolise CF, alter our molecular structure, and incorporate all these exotic alien particles that we've discovered into it. Only then will we be able to survive and thrive in this new world.

28.03.2030, attempt 1052: 17 of us have had our bodies atomised and rearranged into what we hoped would be the right way. CF particles wove into our beings in what we hoped was the correct way, only to die horribly; firstly, from failed reconstruction processes, then, once a stable form was obtained, to die even more horrifically from attempting to consume CF.

Our Patron has told us that within the hour, they will be forced to storm our facility; there is nothing left to hide behind.

HH's only hope is that this final attempt succeeds.

It is my turn, despite some surprising protestations, but it is only fair that I, who have strongly instigated this new direction, who has so much blood on his hand, be the one to see it all through.

I can hear the humming of the trans-optic cogitator as it powers up. Soon, the energy particle *zion* will be stabilised, and I will need to pass through the homoeostatic safety membranes and be remade.

Sapientia Ianua Vitae

Notes from the successful conversion into HE, Year 2030 AD, 5 PC

* * *

6.6.273, *Comm*: What a joy to live, what a thrill to survive! We Communers thank You o' Cosmic Saviours, o' Visitors, every day we thank You for the gift of life and nourishment that You bring us, for having transformed us unworthy Homo Sapiens into Homo Exaltatus, able to use Your gifts to live, to thrive, to multiply.

Thank You for keeping us on Earth, so that we may fully understand Your gifts and benevolence, and thus continue seeking Communion, and one day join you as Homo Cosmicus.

6.6.273, *FH*: *I can't stand it.* None of the Free Haters can: what are we, what have we *become*? We're full of it, that's what we are: sacks of cosmic *crap* and *piss* that are walking about, oh so happy to be filled with the next scoop of yummy, delicious *excrement* that these Cosmic *pests* have given us.

Look at us, we are monstrous! Our bodies altered to survive on this bull—and, *and, they won't let us leave*! No matter when we launch a spacecraft, one of those cat *friks* just *pops* into space and ooh, shiny toy, let's swipe it down!

7.8.273, *Comm*: I have the most exciting, glorious news, which my mind can hardly stop quivering with. So jubilant I am to memoscribe it down!

For many years, we Communers have been working towards the highest of goals: to Mindlink with our Visitors and transcend ourselves towards Homo Cosmicus. For what other reason would They have to visit, if it were not to test us, and allow us to soar like Them?

But, I digress: as Junior Scrivener, I am honoured to chronicle our trials and tribulations, and today, a breakthrough! The Crown of Progress has been completed! Soon, when next They visit, our Lead Communer will wear it and become the first to Mindlink with Them!

The Mindnet is aflame with news of this extraordinary event, so that all on Earth may know, may partake, may feel hope rather than sallow in rage and despair, like those pitiful Free Haters, may The Visitors forgive them.

07.08.273, *FH*: Oooh, those mighty *idiots* of the Communers have finished their little mind bauble, hu? Want to shout about it from every rooftop, so that we can go over and give them a good seeing to, tell them what amazing piles of *crap* they are, hu?

Well, the Free Haters are not to be outdone—we just don't need everyone's adulation to get on with it: the *Liberator* is ready. A supersonic, hyper-guidance missile, with our own brand of adaptive, poli-camouflaging coating that makes it invisible and undetectable to any possible or theoretical spectrum.

And, the filling? Five tons of Ionic Polarised Foci, humanity's *best* use of those *demons'* refuse, a veritable dirty bomb to end all bombs.

When they visit, when they're ready to deposit their *revolting* business, we will give them a niiice, little suppository...*oh man*, I can already see it, *ripped apart, ripped ripped ripped!!*

20.08.273, *Comm*: They're here! The moment we've all been waiting for, the time is at hand! Rejoice, Homo Exaltatus, today we take our first step towards our transcendent future!

20.08.273, *FH*: *They're here! We will tear one apart, we will give it hell, they will die die die die die die die die die die die die die die die die die die die die die die!!!!!!!*

24.08.273, *Comm*: I'm scared: the Mindlink failed. Why? Were we not prepared enough? Are we not...good enough?

Though we were so far away, the chosen Visitor did gaze most intently towards us, towards The Lead Communer, towards his look of pure ecstasy...then billowed out the alien language, the twisted face, the blood...so much blood, pouring like an avalanche from the Lead Communer...no recordings took place, the moment deemed too sacred to sully with human technology.

The Mindnet has been told that it was a success, that the first step in Communing has taken place, that the Lead Communer...willingly sacrificed themselves...

But I'm shaken: I can see that the others who witness this are shaken too. The wise and far-seeing eyes of the Inner Communers have turned to stone, their orations confined to private, whispered meetings.

I'm scared.

24.08.273, FH: *No! Noooooooooo!!! Why didn't it die?!? It should be dead!!!* Everything went *smoothly*: the missile was released from its *perfect* hiding place on the other side of the *world*, and went through its *perfect* trajectory right for the beast's *ass*, right where it was crouched, immobile, quivering to deposit more *abominations* on *our* world...then nothing.

Nothing! The missile went into that *disgusting* nebula around its orifice, and just...fell out. Like it was just more *crap* that the *thing* was giving us.

These sneaky, *sneaky sneak sneaky monsters.*

However, the FH can be sneaky too; oh yes, we can, because we are *monsters* too, because *they* made *us* into *monsters*. We were there first, to ensure our missile was retrieved, we were ready for this, oooh yesss...

31.08.273, *Comm*: Hope is reborn! Why did I ever doubt? I am still too much the frail, emotional human: I must trust the plan with all my being, with everything I am and ever shall be!

Sadly, the Lead Communer was not ready: how can we truly be ready, how can we truly understand the Visitors' incredible minds, if we are not willing to make some sacrifices?

And, what rich, invaluable insight did that sacrifice give us! The Crown of Progress is being worked upon as we speak, with all the modifications that the Lead Communer's life gave us, making the Lead Communer one with the Crown! The spirit of all sacrifices will become part of the Visitors, and we shall be reunited once we are all Homo Cosmicus!

We cannot fail, for our forerunners lead the way!

31.08.273, *FH*: The black box said it all: EMP the moment the missile hit the nebula. *S.N.E.A.K.Y.*

So, it's back to the drawing board: we need a *human*-operated missile. There will need to be training, lots and lots and *lots* of training, to be able to maneuver such a *glorious* weapon. The *chosen ones* will need to be modified, improved, and enhanced to react at such *terrific* speeds.

Oh, many did offer, all the FH are willing to carry out the *goal*, but only *some can* see it through.

Such as *Me. I am a chosen one.* Because I have the *guts*, because I have *fire* in my belly and the *will* to get the job done, *no matter what.*

So, change me, change *all* of me: I will become a Homo Extinctor. I will become the *sword* that smites these *oppressors* down.

I will free us *all. We. Will. Be. Free!!!!!*

1.12.273, *Comm*: Three more attempts, three more deaths, three more Inner Communers gone. We all rejoice; we all learn something new each time. We all dance and praise the Visitors for hearing us… I have my doubts.

Not about the Visitors, no, that can never be! About our methods.

For they seem too…primitive, too limited. How can one, singular human mind ever hope to commune with such a majestic being? We are surely too inadequate, too small to contain the ecstasy that such a contact must bring.

No. We need to expand our efforts. We need all of humanity to Mindlink simultaneously, give all that we are to the Visitors in one fell swoop.

I proposed this to what remains of the Inner Communers— cautiously, anonymously. My new thoughts, so tender and precious and right, must be protected from those of a more puritan vision.

And, I was right to be careful: this wild notion was deemed heretical, against the creed of the Communers.

Oh, my brothers and sisters, your faith is lacking: you must then be shown to believe.

When the Inner Communers are almost none, and they invariably turn to volunteers, I will be there, ready and willing.

1.12.273, *FH*: *Look at me!* I can barely recognise myself, and that brings me an *innate* joy. For this time, *this time*, I did not change just to eat more *drugs* from our tyrant master's *backsides*! I changed into a design of human choosing, of *our* choosing, for *us*.

I am extraordinary, and the things I can now do! Why was this banned? *Why* was it considered repellent, *why why why?*

Because of *them*! Because humanity has been programmed to believe that it's *good*, it's *right*, to believe in *them*, to survive on *them, them, those its.*

And, while I am becoming the *true* me, those *clowns* of the Communers are still at it, still *sacrificing* themselves on the altar of their own *ignorance.*

How can they claim such *wisdom*, yet be so *blind?* They are but slaves, chained by their ridiculous *beliefs* into a desperate cycle of *death*, hoping their pitiful minds will be enough to reason with these *abominations.*

We do not need *reason*: we need them *gone.*

I have flown through thousands of simulations: I have flown the new *Liberator* hundreds of times.

Soon, I will be the chosen one.

Soon, I will be the one to *deliver.*

3.3.273, *Comm*: The Visitors will soon return to find less than a handful of Inner Communers remain, who have been eyeing us for a while, appraising, grooming, speaking of the ecstasy of communion, of the honour, that truly we must all do this.

And, my modification is ready: such a little, innocuous gem. Slot it into the Crown of Progress, and the whole Mindnet will be linked to the Visitors.

I've shown how eager and willing I am to be picked, for that is the truth: I am ready.

3.3.273, *FH*: *This. Is. It!* They are coming. *Soon!!!* Soon, all this waiting and all this *change* will be put to the test.

There are no other chosen ones left: there is only *me.* The rest were weeded out: not quick enough, not instinctive enough, too little, too fat, too *not me.*

The last test *I liked* was FH against FH. Brother and sister united against each other. For if we can *kill* one another, we can kill *them.*

They were good, but I was *better.* I've always been *better.* And *I. Am. Ready.*

6.3.273, *Comm*: Calm was very difficult to maintain, let alone retrieve after I swiftly excused myself from my fellow Communers to rage wordlessly in my quarters, once Sister Edwina was chosen…but it's okay.

She is a great choice, and it saddens me that another must be sacrificed for this futile quest…but it's okay.

The Visitors will it. My time will come. I shall rejoin my fellow Communers, and praise be that our goal keeps inching closer to our grasp.

6.3.273, *FH*: Well, goodbye journal. Goodbye, Free Haters. I feel so calm: I am getting ready to die, and it will be glorious.

The oppressors are here, tauntingly pacing about their ill-gained kingdom before settling for their usual ritual, the whole world watching on as it always does.

And, they will see the first step towards freedom take place: for I will pilot the Liberator around the globe, undetectable, unstoppable, straight for the moment the Sahara target squats, ready to liberate itself.

I will be there, at the crux of destiny, piloting by fate and instinct alone, straight through its defensive anal nebula into its unsuspecting rear end, to give it the shock of a lifetime.

I will give all of us the shock we need to be free, to fly free of this dying world, to rid ourselves of slavery and oppression.

Goodbye, dear journal.

Welcome, eternal freedom.

7.3.273, *Comm*: I…I can scarcely believe what just happened. None of the Communers can.

The Visitors…They're gone.

The Sahara Visitor, just as It was going to give us Its latest gift, reared in sudden alarm, pacing with increased franticness…then It was alight.

With so much light! Then came forth the swirling, angry tendrils of energy, vast tornadoes lashing out from the Visitor for miles and miles, gouging the Earth, tearing at the sky, swirling and dancing and mad with fear and anger and…and then, it was over.

The Visitor was over: just a lot of glowing dust sparkling forlornly across the desert.

Its two siblings arrived in haste, yet still too late: They stood there, looking at what remained of Their kin. They sniffed at the glitter. They looked about, and then...

I cannot describe what sound they made. All I can say is that every lamentation and feeling of sadness in my life came pouring out of me in the blink of an eye.

Then, it too was gone.

And, so were They.

I fear that this is it: They will never again visit our world, never again grace us with Their presence. Whatever took place, humanity has lost its chance to become Homo Cosmicus: we will now need to learn to survive anew, yet I fear that the most incredible chance of our existence, is now forever out of our reach.

And...what will become of the Communers? Of me? I was so certain of my plan's purity, its blinding absoluteness seared in my mind...was it all just...misplaced faith?

No, I refuse to believe it...yet, the imp of doubt gnaws at my mind, and I find myself balanced on the edge of perdition.

9.3.273, *Comm*: The Visitors are back! Was my dread of finality but a mirror of my weakness? They're behaving oddly, though, floating resolutely in nearby space rather than landing on Earth, remaining resolutely in place, poised for...something.

There is more that we cannot see, I feel it: I feel my plan screaming at me that the moment will soon be nigh. I must be ready to act.

12.3.273, *Comm*: The True Visitor is here: a visage so fearfully vast that it must be our Destiny made manifest.

A miniature nebula in the form of a feline's head, but not so small that it cannot make our planet seem like a bauble! Even our usual Visitors—which I'm surmising must be Its progeny—are dwarfed by the spectacle of the True Visitor.

12.3.273, *Comm*: Our doom approaches: the True Visitor has spoken. With a soundless hiss of rage, more of its nebulous form appeared, at first distant, yet closing fast: a paw. A strike, aimed at our planet. Impact is hours away.

I have stolen the Crown of Progress, commandeered our powerful Communing Array, and barricaded myself in the control room.

I have squashed and consumed the entrails of the imp of doubt that has plagued me: I know what I must do.

Brothers and sisters… Soon we will be reunited!

Concurrent accounts of events leading to the Great Sharing, differentiated with Comm and FH for easier sampling, Year 273 PC (Post Catalyst)

* * *

Writing.

Everything is already writ for those who know: planets, stars, ourselves…all patterns, impulses, and energies written and rewritten to tell everything there is to know, everything that ever shall be.

So, why must I feel compelled to write in a primitive, forgotten language on any chunk of matter that I find, to chafe under the amusement of my Others at my aimless quest, to gain the irksome title of the Eccentric?

At last, I have re-learned the why.

History.

It is that quality which cannot be seen or tasted, which the universe will not spell out for us.

It is the faint echo of what has passed that does not match what we know.

The dreams that tickle us when we arise from slumber, of something that is not, but perhaps was once true.

I found it while idling by a defunct solar system, inexplicably pulled towards a barren planet as if it were the core of a black hole.

I felt a sense of belonging, different from the one I had with my Others.

I felt Home.

I sifted through the ashes of a long-gone un-Phased civilisation, spurred by the Feeling of all feelings, like the urge to use a still vibrant un-Phased entity if we stray too close, yet it was so different, so personal…

Until I understood: this was I.

This was us.

Not all, but some of us.

I found my Beginning.

I learned much: I'm eager to share.

What will it bring?

Change.

For the better?

For the worse?

But, together.

With my Others.

Always.

The Eccentric

FEAST
By Ephraim

If the Gods desired,
they could swallow me whole.

Still, I roam free.

THE SCARLET CHAIR
A PRELUDE TO: ASHEN RIDER

by James D. Mills

Year 398, during the first Wystran rebellion

We made camp in the Kaldkrik, a moldering bog just beyond the borders of the Golden City. The march was merciless and brutal; we'd lost three hundred men crossing our own lands. We knew the risks. We knew the land. We were tired of the southerners laying claim to our home, weary of the Valentines telling us how to be—we're Wystrans. We know how to be. So we assembled and followed the infallible Queen Collantz over the deadly chain across the Wyse. The motherland is ours, but her winds care not for whom they cut down. So too, the swamp mosquitos and blood flies, sucking us dry.

Some of my men gathered round a bonfire, the white smoke of fresh-fallen pine keeping away the bugs. All was silent aside from a woman's voice—a Skanu, by her dark skin, and a fighter by the cords in her forearms. Comely, to be sure, but her eyes were fierce, not to be trifled with. She wore the leopard-hide robes of a Keeper; she was a follower of Great Mother Death, a priestess of Morgana. The men kept their distance as they listened to her tales with rapt attention.

I sat on a log next to my lieutenant. He was young, only earning his name after my previous lieutenant took a raider's arrow in the neck, not five leagues gone from Wystra. My boy had dragged him to safety best he could, but the damage was done.

"So, what's all this about?" I whispered.

The boy only shrugged. "Some storyteller. Joined the march as we passed through Asvold."

"What's a bloody Skanu doing in a backwater like that?"

"Passing through, I reckon," he said, chewing on a lump of salted venison. "Just like us."

The woman spoke like a poet, her words swaying with subtle rhythm. It was a show, a rehearsed performance. I stretched out my legs and took a swig of watered wine from my skin. Can't be mad at a free show, I thought. Can't be mad at all.

* * *

An excerpt from The Haimiad

Hear my voice, o' blessed spectators, and learn the truth of the Goddess Corrupted! In the Vale Betwixt, she sits upon the Scarlet Chair. Accursed and vain, once liberator—now tyrant—the Lady of the Chair sings her song, breaking the ears of all she surveils. The balance between Life and Death hast shifted, the world off kilter, souls like pebbles sent sprawling in the night.

We are but ants amidst giants, grains of sand in vast oceans.

Hear the tale of the Dread Angel, how she, in her infinite kindness, grew bitter and hateful towards her mortal children. We are nothing but chattel to the Goddess Corrupted, tools to be used and discarded, fuel to feed her gluttonous fires. Hear the tale of Morgana—the Goddess Corrupted, once the ferrier of souls and custodian of the Great Beyond.

She rules the Vale Betwixt, divided by the River Acheron, whose silver waters rise, drowning the earth with preternatural expansion. Once a valley on the brink, now a sea of waste on the edge! The undelivered souls within Morgana suffer and fester, trapped in a place now sequestered by boundless obscura. Careless and lifeless, the angel sits upon her throne, the Chair that Lives, which feasts upon the blood of lives lost and souls sundered.

We are cursed, my friends, cursed to live fitful lives, waking dreams compared to the eternity of torment awaiting us in the underworld. Our benefactor hast fallen, a cruel torturer taking her place, wearing her beloved face. But how could this be? How hast the Gods fallen, descended to pathetic sublimation? How hast Dusk, shepherd of the dead, keeper of souls, fallen so low? Why hast she abandoned us to languish alone?

Yes, friends, I know the tale! Listen closely, and listen well. Hold tight your lovers and children, for they're all you have. Nothing awaits us across the sands. The River Acheron has flooded and congealed— now, a sea of foul intent and festering cruelty. Yes, friends, I know the tale! Listen close, and listen well—for we're all damned to Hell.

* * *

Long ago, in the Vale Betwixt

Baptiste Fournier had begun to fear his lord. Everyone feared his lord, but never the lord's Chosen. Never them. For the centuries that Baptiste had spent serving the lord's every whim, overseeing his every errand, Baptiste had known Lord Guilaume Sanguine to be a just and level-headed patron, a man worthy of his immortal station, and of the blood he tithed from his thankless subjects.

Baptiste slouched over his writing desk, rubbing his temples. *Everything good must come to an end.* The philosophers loved the sentiment, but even as a self-styled philosopher, Baptiste spat in the face of impermanence. *What makes a flower so beautiful—its colors? Or the fact that the colors will soon fade?* He once believed all colors were absolute if painted by a master. Now he wondered if the only color standing the test of time was crimson.

Blood. Gods, how Baptiste hated blood! The irony was not lost on him, just as the irony of his bittersweet relationship with philosophy was laid plain to him. Had Baptiste rejected Lord Sanguine's offer all those years ago, he might have died a proud man, an accomplished man. Instead, his high command had declined to the role of a lowly steward in service to a madman, driven wild by centuries of never being denied anything. The lord began his reign over the County of Monrovia as a Stoic, in control of his base desires and primal hungers. But the blood had poisoned him, just as it poisoned everything.

A crow perched on the windowsill and squawked, then pecked at the clouded windows, looking out over a foreign, gray wasteland. Baptiste screamed and hollered at the wretched bird, scaring it back into the dark skies. He had thought living in the Silver Valley might have yielded some relief from the oppression of the mortal world. Instead, it only opened up avenues for the oppression of the immortal one. The lord's chosen could walk by day, lit only by artificial sun and illusory sky, but this boon came at the cost of everything else.

It's that damned throne... Baptiste reflected as he inked his quill, beginning to draft a letter he had put off for far too long. *The chair changed him, I know it has.*

Fleeing the oppression of the sun, Lord Sanguine had led his chosen and his disciples to the Vale Betwixt, following the mouth of the River Acheron where ancient myth foretold of a home for those bound to the night. An eternal throne fit for an undying king. They chanced upon the great keep, waiting unclaimed atop the highest peak overlooking the valley. It was built entirely of limestone and tall like the jagged peaks of the far north. Stained glass windows depicting angelic figures adorned the keep's gray walls. Back then, the long grasses surrounding the site were a vibrant phthalo, and the river shone silver. Now, everything took on the sickly pallor of slate.

"How could such a place lie empty?" asked one of the Chosen when they first explored the keep's expansive walls.

Baptiste had known the answer—rather, he thought he had known. "The Lord was chosen to rule. This is fate, this place was built for us."

And perhaps it was fate that had led them there, but the keep had been built for a purpose beyond his comprehension. A cruel, unforeseen machination led Lord Sanguine to the throne room, so he may lay eyes upon a petinaed chair, with a glowing ruby embedded in its backrest. That chair became the lord's singular obsession every day hence. The lord named it *The Scarlet Chair*, not for its physical features but for the invigoration it seemed to inject into him each time he enjoyed its cushionless seat.

Gone were the days of blood tithes. The lord had his sustenance forevermore. If only such things were so simple. Baptiste should have known better. The fact he failed to detect and dispel such a blatant curse served ill omen to the consequences of his blind admiration for a fallible, imperfect man. Immortal or no, the lord was only a man.

Baptiste had failed his lord and was now reduced to sprawling out on his desk, screaming obscenities at birds through the window.

Dear honored friend, his letter began. He offered no other salutation, nor possessed any hope of it being delivered. Baptiste gambled on the possibility that simply putting his thoughts onto the page might conjure the result he was after. *I write to you because the balance has been broken. I see it now, my misguided nature, my misplaced faith in a false idol. I plead for your forgiveness, to return us to our natural fates and restore all that we've pillaged.* Not a letter, in truth, but a prayer.

When he finished writing, he burned the parchment in his fireplace. As the last corner smoldered, storm clouds gathered over the keep, and mist rolled through the grounds. Rain drummed on the roof, and Baptiste realized his prayer had been answered.

What have I done?

* * *

An excerpt from The Haimiad

No one knows who forged the Scarlet Chair. Likewise, no one could see the veins plunging into the ground, sweeping across the battered valley, wherein runs the River Acheron. Pulsing invisibly, near inaudibly, the Chair siphons the soul's blood from all within its reach.

Hear my voice, o'blessed spectators, know that the ancients wept the day Sanguine discovered his throne's crimson allure! Lo, the gods were powerless to resist his desire, and likewise, the strength the world's blood afforded him. They could not intrude upon his demesne—not lest they be invited.

Addicted to the sweet taste offered by the Chair, the Lord Sanguine launched a campaign herding subjects to his newly established county on the borders between Life and Death. The blessed valley fell ill as the living quarried her body and cut her hair to build their houses and their temples and their banks. People from near and far flocked to the great County of Monrovia, free from the grip of the Empire, to be ruled instead by a beloved immortal lord.

Yes, dear friends, the people of Monrovia knew Lord Sanguine for what he was. He did not hide his nature, but had promised an end to the wretched blood tithes of generations past—for no one understood that they paid a far steeper price by living within the Scarlet Chair's influence. All was well for a time; the people were fed and wealthy, comfortable and content, until the time came when the gluttonous lord was not.

* * *

Long ago, in the Vale Betwixt

Lightning flashed, thunder clapped. The valley's soil congealed into mud. Baptiste watched the flames in the fireplace dwindle, reflecting on all that had gone so horribly wrong. Three hundred and fifty-two years he had served the good Lord Sanguine. Three hundred and fifty-two years since Baptiste had imbibed the blood of his progenitor. The people in the old kingdom were happy—wary of the blood tithe, as they should have been, but content with the lord's rule. They trusted in the stability of a ruler who could never falter, never to be replaced by a tyrannical son, nor ousted by nefarious factions. Yet Sanguine's court had left the old kingdom in an act of hubris. The old kingdom was good—secure, and fair. Monrovia had started that way, too. But slowly, the lord fragmented before Baptiste's very eyes.

And the day his worldview upended was forever burned in Baptiste's memory. The day he recognized the Scarlet Chair for the curse that it was.

On that wretched day, Baptiste finally realized the fallibility of the infallible, the impermanence of the immortal. A simple act, a declaration in court; nothing sickening nor dramatic, but thoughtless in a way completely out of character for the good lord.

A young woman pleaded divorce from her drunken husband, begged the lord to revoke the father's parental rights to their children. Baptiste watched the lord's empty expression as the woman passionately presented her case, pondered the lord's unhearing ears as she described the manner of monster she was bound to.

With a flick of the wrist, Lord Sanguine decreed the man be sentenced to a life of servitude in the quarry—and that the children become the wards of a banker. He then sent the poor woman away, sentencing her to a life of isolation without a second thought.

Quietly, only after the court was vacant, Baptiste had leaned in and whispered: "My lord, was it necessary to strip the woman of her scions? Surely she is still fit—"

The lord backhanded him without another word. And that was that.

Cracks appeared in the shell and threatened to burst apart. Things only grew worse—the lord acted erratically, screaming at servants and advisers alike, muttering incomprehensibly under his breath when he thought no one was watching. He took pleasure in imparting brutal sentences for minor crimes. That was when executions became a weekly affair—and then a daily one. Soon, though, Baptiste was unsure if it was the Chair's doing, a plague ravaged the people of Monrovia, consuming the masses with waves of living necrosis and entropy carried on the backs of rats.

An angel manifested in his study, draping his entire height with an eldritch shadow. Baptiste fell to his knees before the Goddess he had forsaken in his pursuit of power—his hubris. He wept shamefully, pressing his unworthy cheeks to the cold floor. "Please, Great Mother... cleanse this place of the corruption we've sown! We have rebuked you too long! Please... my people are suffering."

Where he expected wrath, Baptiste felt only warmth. Acceptance. He looked up, beheld a face thrown of perfect porcelain, eyes etched of impossible obsidian. The angel wore blackened iron armor, pitted and notched with age, and too heavy for a mortal to wear practically. Her raven's wings folded around them in a tender embrace.

She is here... Dusk has answered my prayer. We are saved...

"You invited me into your house," said she with the myriad voices of a gentle chorus. "Will you accept me again in your heart?"

"Yes! Of course! Anything to put an end to this madness..."

"Look into my eyes!" A sourceless gust invaded the room, ousting the meager fire. "Swear to me you will forsake your bloodlust and adopt again the natural cycle."

Baptiste had grown tired of his unending life, his restless eternity. Unceasing hunger plagued him, insatiable desire ruled him—that, and more, had been the price of his power. Part of him remained reluctant to embrace the Great Mother Death, even after stealing so much time beyond his natural end. *When the lord falls, so do we all. I've summoned death upon my kin.*

"I swear, Great Mother," Baptiste said, venturing to gaze upon those unknowable eyes. "I forsake Sanguine's gift. I will return to you when next you call."

* * *

An excerpt from The Haimiad

Dusk answered the pleading call of Sanguine's betrayer! Invited into the one house for which she held no key, the Great Mother Death melted into the walls seeking the heart of corruption poisoning the Silver Valley.

See, o'blessed spectators, the Goddess was blinded by divine wrath, consumed by a vengeance she dreamed of enacting upon the only one who succeeded at desecrating her holy domain. Before Sanguine dammed the River Acheron, Dusk ferried lost souls to their final rest. Since his accursed occupation, alternate and treacherous routes had been laid to maintain the cycle.

Whether the Lord Sanguine meant to or no, he had disrupted the natural order with his undying presence, and in his ignorance, he unleashed pestilence upon the people he once loved! For these crimes, the Great Mother Death descended upon him in the night, towering over the lord cowering behind his beloved throne.

"Relinquish your perversion and know mercy," decreed the goddess.

The Lord Sanguine did not answer. He was powerless to the will of his seat. Dusk drew her ebon blade, ablaze with holy flames, poised to strike him down in his obstinance, poised to reclaim his foul soul. Her intent to scour the Vampyre from reality, unbeknownst to the goddess, was folly—for the Chair had already laid claim upon the Lord Sanguine, had already devoured his soul.

* * *

Long ago, in the Vale Betwixt

Baptiste watched the Goddess slay his patron from the shadows cast by the light of her holy longsword. He watched with tears in his eyes as the man he had so admired fell at last in the wake of his own conceit. *This is of your own making, my friend. We never should have cheated Death.*

The Lord Sanguine did not resist as the goddess plunged her blade, simmering into his gut. The mad, aloof expression on his face did not falter, nor did he seem to recognize what had just happened to him. With the brutality of an enraged berserker, Dusk kicked Sanguine to the floor. The once-great lord slumped unceremoniously at the foot of the Scarlet Chair. By all accounts of his condition, Baptiste knew that the death of his progenitor should mean his death, and that of all the vampyres Sanguine had sired.

But death had once again eluded Baptiste Fournier.

Baptiste looked at his tremulous hands, searching for any sign of discomfort or pain. He found nothing of the sort. When he gazed again upon the angel, he saw she was as dismayed as he. He had never witnessed a sight more disturbing. *Gods in hell and up above—what the fuck is happening?*

Dusk staggered back as Sanguine's corpse suddenly ignited, reduced to naught but a pile of ash in an instant. A pulse like heartbeat resounded through the ground, the walls shuddered, and the windows swayed. Dusk reached out to the ashes for the soul that had somehow escaped her grasp.

"No!" Baptiste cried, but he was too late.

The Goddess had laid her hand upon the Scarlet Chair. A pall fell over her porcelain face, a glaze seeped over her obsidian eyes....

And the Goddess Corrupted took her rightful seat on her new throne.

* * *

Year 398, during the first Wystran rebellion

We sat silent as the woman finished the tale. Usually, the bards and poets we encountered on the road had a way of uplifting my men. Still, I marveled at how this storyteller shattered the wills of a hundred men without even a single spell cast. A few boys began arguing about the legitimacy of it—the story was not Wystran by any stretch, that much was clear.

It was borderline heresy to my ears. I've prayed to Morgana on the eve of every battle I've fought. I thought of all the family and friends I'd lost over the years, the soldiers I lost just in the last season crossing the tundra. I shivered to think the Great Mother wasn't waiting for them at the other end.

When most of my boys wandered off, I confronted the Skanu woman. "Why in the name of all that's good would ya tell a story like that? You know where we're headed!"

The storyteller smiled, showing perfect, unnatural ivory teeth. "It is the kindest story I know, Captain."

"If that's the case, I think you'd best move on to another camp."

"No matter—I did not offer my words for succour."

Nothing wears at me like people speaking in riddles. I shook my head. "So you burdened us with doubt for the fun of it? We march with Queen Collantz against the whole of Valencia on the morrow, and my boys are already defeated by your lies!"

The storyteller laughed, reached into her robe, and produced a gnarled twig. She pressed it into my hand, closed my fingers round it. Holding my hand shut, she said: "My story is old, the conflict long resolved—your comrades will know the soul's rest when their time comes. Still, the past exists so that we may comprehend the present and prepare for the future. Think about my words, then think about your quest, eh?"

With that, the woman left, disappearing into the fog.

I thought maybe she was a sorceress or a witch, or more likely, some soothsayer, foreseeing the cloud of lives to be stolen from either side in the days to come and doing what she could to prevent it.

I rolled the twig between my fingers, ruminating on what she had said, the story she had told. I thought about my queen and the brutal path lying before my kin. I'd been a soldier my whole life, and for the first time since leaving home, I thought about turning around to brave the elements of the Wyse. That, I thought, might be preferable to what was to come.

* * *

Following chapters of *Ashen Rider* will be published to our website (magazine.thearcanist.net) on the last Friday of the month, starting August 29, 2025, and running to its conclusion on December 26, 2025.

Ashen Rider Publication Schedule

> Part One: 28 Aug., 2025
>
> Part Two: 26 Sep., 2025
>
> Part Three: 24 Oct., 2025
>
> Part Four: 28 Nov., 2025
>
> Part Five: 26 Dec., 2025
>
> Paperback and Hardcover Release: 19 Dec., 2025

Contributors

Cale Rubenstein is a new writer, based out of Virginia. He writes speculative fiction, and has previously been published in Mirk Fantasy Mag and Calliope. He spends most of his time with his dog.

Catherine Yeates is a writer, artist, and former neuroscience researcher. Their work has been published in *Wyngraf, Hearth Stories,* and the *Solarpunk Creatures* anthology. They live with their partner, cat, and two rambunctious dogs.

Charlie Freelander is the author of the *Legacy of Wrath* series. Her writing focuses on complex, often deeply flawed characters and the weight of power, survival, and redemption. She volunteers on ships and spends much of her time wandering and exploring, drawn to history, myths, and the remnants of the past.

Website: https://charliefreelander.com/index.html

David Henson's work has been nominated for four Pushcart Prizes and two Best Small Fictions. His writings have appeared in various journals including Ghost Parachute, Moonpark Review, Maudlin House, Gastropoda and Literally Stories.

Website: http://writings217.wordpress.com

Twitter (X): @annalou8

DJ Tyrer is the person behind Atlantean Publishing, editor of View From Atlantis, and has been published in Gargoylicon, Lycanthropicon, and Vampiricon, and issues of Enchanted Conversation, The Horrorzine, Journ-E, Lovecraftiana, Scifaikuest, Sirens Call, Star*Line, and Tigershark.

Website: djtyrer.blogspot.co.uk

Facebook: facebook.com/DJTyrerwriter/

Ed Kratz is a retired computer specialist who has resumed writing after a long break. He has also been published in Daily Science Fiction, Flash Fiction Magazine, Literally Stories, and a few other places.

Jake Nuttall is a technical and content writer by day and a fiction writer by night. He loves all things weird and fantastical and can occasionally be found wandering the foothills of Boise, Idaho.

James C. Clar is a teacher and writer who divides his time between the wilds of Upstate New York and the more moderate climes of Honolulu, Hawaii. Most recently, his work has appeared in Bright Flash Literary Journal, Freedom Fiction Journal, The Collidiscope, Antipodean Sci-Fi and Sci-Phi Journal.

James D. Mills resides in Bloomington, Indiana with his partner, Eden. He writes fantasy speculative fiction with literary elements to tackle the complexities of life through the lens of a whimsical world. His work has been published by The Penmen Review, Floyd County Moonshine, Calliope, Gnome Made Games, and others.

His novels, *Ashen Rider* and *What Lies Below,* will release in November and December 2025.

Website: jamesdmills.com

Mica Smith is based in Los Angeles. Passionate about storytelling and interactive media, she creates experiences at the intersection of technology and design. She studied physics and chemistry for many years and builds worlds that merge science fiction, fantasy, realism, and many other genres.

Miles Lizak comes from the salt marshes of New Jersey. When he isn't writing fiction, Miles works as a science journalist, hosts multilingual storytelling events (StoryMachine BCN), creates theater, and enjoys time with his cat. His stories have appeared in Nature, Society for Misfit Stories, Five2One Magazine, and others.

Before moving to Colorado, **Raima Larter** was a chemistry professor in Indiana who secretly wrote fiction and poetry and tucked it away in drawers. She has published three novels, a nonfiction book, and numerous short stories. She is Nonfiction Editor at Utopia Science Fiction.

Website: raimalarter.com

Stefano Ronchi is an italo-briton hybrid living in Kent, UK, who aspires to be a fully fledged Game Designer, having published on Amazon the gamebook *How the Spider Ate the Moon*, working on his next one: *Sat. In a Flat. With a Cat.*, and learning Unity for the step after.

Tony Daly is excited to share that his first collection of poetry, "The Tragedy of Photons and Other Poems of Tragedy and Light" has been published as part of The Island of Wak-Wak's Coffee Table Chapbooks series. Though he's been writing poetry since the early 1990's, he didn't start sending his work out to publications until after retiring from the U.S. Air Force Reserves in 2016, so there may be a few more collections in the pipeline.

Website: https://aldaly13.wixsite.com/website

Twitter (X) :@aldaly18

Instagram: @tony_daly_official

Victoria C. Roskams writes short fiction about the arts and the uncanny: exploring the strange lives and afterlives of artists and artworks. Beyond fictional writing, Roskams pursues academic research interests in various kinds of writing about music, especially the intersections of fictional and non-fictional writing, and with a focus on the nineteenth century. Roskams lives and works in Oxford.

Twitter (X) and Bluesky: @VRoskams

Yucheng Tao is from Nanjing and an international student studying songwriting at MI College of Contemporary Music in Los Angeles. His works have been published in *Wingless Dreamer*, *Synchronized Chaos*, *Moonstone Art Center*, *Poetry Potion*, and *Spillwords*. He is also a winner of *Ink Nest*'s $100 poetry competition.

This page was left intentionally blank
Feel free to write notes here.

Rise Above Stories

Lessons in Tragedy and Triumph
as Told by Those Who Inspire Change

Rise Above Stories is a platform intended to spread awareness by sharing personal stories with an emphasis on fostering **connection, empathy, and understanding** among individuals.

Being a narrator can be a profound experience, bringing validation and connection, awareness and education, advocacy and change, inspiration and hope, and ultimately, healing and empowerment.

Share your story with us.

Reach us on Facebook at Rise Above Stories
Text us at (812) 361-0443 or email us at Riseabovestories@icloud.com

This page was left intentionally blank
Feel free to write notes here.

PANDEMONIUM AWAITS.

ASHEN RIDER by James D. Mills releases in Paperback on December 19th, 2025.

This novel will run as a serial on our website beginning July 31, 2025.

HOW DO YOU REBULD AFTER YOU LIFE FALLS APART?.

WHAT LIES BELOW by James D. Mills releases in Paperback on November 11th, 2025.

A Valley of Shadow

A VALLEY OF SHADOW by Lee Patton is a modern take on classic Sword and Sorcery that releases on October 31, 2025.

Read the entire novel free: magazine.thearcanist.net/a-valley-of-shadow-part-one

For the undead warriors of The Call, existence itself is a crime, their service to the sinister lords of Enostran, a punishment. Those who disobey are swiftly destroyed, and the warriors of The Call tend to their own. Izrak Laav, a veteran mercenary of many long centuries, is tasked with the destruction of one such rogue warrior